THE BOSS

A psychological thriller with a heart-pounding twist

James Caine

PROLOGUE

A good boss doesn't kill their staff.

I stand by the sink, looking at the red stains on my pants suit, blood splattered on my face. I run the faucet, letting the sound of the gushing water mesmerize me.

What had I just done?

This went too far.

It was stupid, I know. It wasn't my fault, though. I take a paper towel and wipe away the blood from my forehead.

What I have done will change everything. Jail is not an option, though.

I look at myself in the mirror, my face nearly clean of the blood. How pathetic do I look? How scared do I seem?

This is not me. I'm confident, overconfident at that. I'm a businesswoman. I exude power. The people who work for me expect me to lead them as I always have. I'm more than respected at the office. People are afraid to be near me.

Not because I'm scary, but because I expect the best out of my staff. I expect the best because

I give the best effort, and others need to show me they will do the same.

That's the attitude that made me climb the corporate ladder at Lovely Beauty Supplies to become president, after all. Executives in Toronto know me. I'm a leader amongst a group of leaders.

I'm Nicole Barrett, dammit. A natural leader. A boss that people can not only look up to but strive to be. I've not only made it to the top of the food chain of Toronto's executive elite, I'm at the forefront.

Me. A woman who came from nothing. I became everything, and at the age of thirty-one.

You don't get to where I am by being weak or lazy. I put in my time every day to be the best, until I was just that.

I regard the pathetic little girl in the mirror who looks scared at the actions she just committed.

This person doesn't show confidence, only fear. This little girl looks like a scared poor child living in squalor with her mother, not a president of a major commercial beauty company.

I hate the little girl staring back at me from the mirror.

I put my hands under the water and find relief in my clean hands, while watching the red go down the drain, taking in a deep breath.

Everything will change now. I look back at the dead body staining the tile floor behind me.

This was not my fault.

It was Alice Walker's fault.
I should have never hired her to begin with.

CHAPTER 1

Alice
Three months prior.

I sit on the couch in our new living room, paralyzed with fear of all the major changes in my life.

I know I should be happy right now. I'm getting everything I ever wanted. Instead, my insecurities have completely taken over my brain. I'm stuck between a feeling of jumping up and down with joy and wanting to curl up in a ball and cry.

Tomorrow is my first day at a Lovely Beauty Supplies, or LBS for short. I'm their new executive director of sales.

My jaw still drops to the floor when I think of my new title.

It took me years to get into a management role when I lived in British Columbia. Next thing I know, I've moved across the country and now I'm a few inches away from being a top executive in an emerging beauty supply company that has huge potential.

Hard work brought me here. I paid my dues to my corporate bosses. I sacrificed a lot of my time and life to get to where I wanted to be, and now the fruits of my labor are paying off.

Evan, my husband, has been supportive of me. He hasn't slowed me down in what I wanted in life, although he can be a good distraction.

We're nearly thirty. He wants to be a father. When we married nearly two years ago, I told him I wanted the same, and I do – but not right now.

Right now, Alice Walker needs to focus on herself. I need to climb the corporate ladder as high as I can go, and once I'm invaluable, once I've proven my worth, I can focus on having a family with Evan.

I'm young and still have plenty of time. Although Evan seems to be going through his midlife crisis much earlier than expected, I'm only twenty-seven. That allows me a lot of time to get to where I need to be.

If you ask Evan, though, he would tell you otherwise. He is obsessed with my eggs and how many of my child rearing years I have left.

He will continue to sneak in statistics of issues older parents have when they have a family later in life.

I'm not worried. When the time comes, I'll make a good mother, I know. I just can't start when I'm at the bottom. I want my children to be raised in an environment where they don't have to worry about money. I want to ensure that I can provide those stable early years for them.

Essentially, I want them to not go through the hell I had growing up.

Evan, while being a good, supportive husband to his overachieving wife, doesn't really help much in that department.

He's currently not working, and that's okay since we just moved to Toronto so that I could start my new job.

Although I tend to set high expectations for myself, I know it's not reasonable for him to move across the country with me and suddenly find work.

What was reasonable, though, was to expect that before we moved to Toronto, he would have a stable career. *Stable* and *career* are not words that are relevant to my husband.

In the working world, we are near opposites. I'm a go-getter, overachiever and will do anything except sell my unborn child to move myself to where I want to be in life. Evan is different.

He won't take any garbage from his superiors. He puts in the work that's required of him and barely anything extra. He gloats about how he quit his last job by telling his boss a four-letter word that starts with F.

Sometimes I can tell he's upset about how successful I am. I never shove it in his face that I make more than him. He knows it. We do our finances together. He sees what I make compared to what he brings in, when he has a job. I don't have to tell him the obvious.

I make enough that he doesn't have to worry about it. I know that a lot of his frustration at the various jobs he's had is that he hasn't found something he's passionate about.

Since I was a girl, I wanted to be an executive at a company. I imagined my name on the outside of a large door in a fancy office, staff working for me, and me leading them.

At one point in his life, I thought Evan had that. He was starting his Bachelors of Education to become a teacher, but dropped out of university in his early twenties. He's struggled to find something he wants to do since.

If he really wants to have a family with me, and with me making more than him, he will likely be the one at home with our future baby more than me. I'll have to return to work early from maternity leave to focus on my career again. He can take on the brunt of what the baby needs.

'You want me to be Mr. Mommy?' Evan asked me once as a joke.

Evan comes up the stairs from the basement, each step squeaking in different tones. He has cut wires in his hand.

"Well, this is a mess," he says. "The electrical wiring is straight out of the 1940s. This wouldn't meet code for sure." He looks at me, waiting for a response, but I just grin.

We knew this place was more than a fixer upper.

Evan found an amazing opportunity, he called it. An older house listed online with an incredible price in a nice area.

The description was nice and fluffy as you would expect. Saying a house is expensive in Toronto is an understatement. This is the most expensive city to live in Canada, even the world for that matter.

We had always wanted a home, and if we were to have a baby sometime in the near future, we wanted to have one in a detached house.

Evan smiles back. "Don't worry, I can handle it," he says confidently.

Although my husband is not confident in the regular workplace, he is certainly handy. His father worked in maintenance and taught his son many different things, from installing flooring even to electrics.

It was something the Walker family would do together. Any house project that was needed to be done, his father would round up Evan and youngest son, Tommy, and they would do it together.

When I got the job at LBS, Evan was happy he would be moving back to where he was raised. He would be close to his brother Tommy again.

Evan's father would have loved working on

renovating this place with him, but unfortunately he passed a year ago. Instead of the Walker family working on a house project together, it would only be Evan and Tommy now.

"When is Tommy coming by to help?" I ask.

"He said he wanted to come tomorrow," Evan says, stuffing the cables in a garbage bag. He already piled up a bunch of debris from things he tore out. Tommy has a truck they can put it in to bring to the dump. "He said he had a few last things he had to do at school before his summer vacation could really begin." He wipes his dirty hands on his jeans.

"Have to love the life of a teacher," I say with a laugh, and immediately regret my words. Sometimes, Evan can be sensitive talking about his brother being a teacher. After all, it was his dream job that he gave up on while his brother succeeded.

"What are you looking at?" Evan asks, nodding at my phone.

"The website of my new company. Lovely Beauty Supplies."

"You're already hired there," Evan says with a chuckle. "You don't have to worry about the company's motto now that the interviews are over. You got the job."

Evan doesn't understand. Your job doesn't end with the interview. It starts the first day, and the next. You need to understand the company's work dynamic, what they want. It's the only way to stay at the top or climb even higher at a company.

The work culture you can learn once you're at the office, but understanding your company, at least the public face of it, is important. At the moment, though, I'm reading the company's About Us page and looking at the numerous faces of corporate positions and who's in them.

One of them I immediately knew. She was the one who hired me. Nicole Barrett. I had never interviewed with the president of a company before and was nervous, but she was extremely friendly, which made it go well.

What made it even better was the amount of preparation I had done before the interview started. Nicole even commented on how well-prepared I was.

I smile at my husband. "I need to refresh what I learned from before. Tomorrow is the first day, and you only have one good chance at first impressions."

"I thought you said your boss seemed nice," he says, confused.

"Well, she is, but it's not just her I need to impress, it's everyone."

Evan turns his head to the side. "You'll be fine."

"I know," I say confidently. "That's why I'm preparing some more."

Evan nods. "You say you'll be fine, but you're doing that thing you do when you're freaking out inside but trying to not show it."

"What?" I say, confused.

"It's your only poker tell I've noticed." He laughs. "If it wasn't for you flaring your nostrils like you're trying to breathe in all the air in the room at once, I would never suspect a thing."

I realize immediately he's right and relax my face.

I sigh and put my phone down. Evan sits on the couch beside me, wrapping his arm around me. "You're going to do just fine tomorrow."

I breathe in deep and rest my head on his shoulder. "I hope you're right."

"You'll see," he says. "And, if for some reason you don't, you can quit. Some other company will be lucky to have my successful wife manage them." He kisses the side of my head.

I don't correct him. It's not that easy. If this doesn't go well, we're totally screwed. I don't explain this to him, though. I wish I had his carefree attitude at times.

Evan takes a hand out of his pocket and a small, rectangular piece of paper falls onto the floor. I see an image of a yellow bell on it, and for a moment worry it's a scratch ticket. Evan used to buy many lottery tickets, and much worse, but he promised he gave that up. Now I see a scratch ticket on the floor?

He picks it up and stares at me, noticing how angry I look. He laughs. "It's just a receipt from the hardware store." He flashes it at me, and I can see the bold letters beside the bell symbol. "Bell Hardware," it reads.

"I'll leave you be," he says as he kisses me again before standing up and going back down the stairs, the steps making different creaking sounds from the kind they made when he came up.

I breathe out and put a finger to my neck, feeling my pulse. It's typically fast but beating out of control at the moment. I slow my breathing and try to calm myself.

I look back down at my cell phone and continue to read the company site, taking in the information about the products they sell and their marketing.

My phone begins to vibrate in my hand from an unknown caller. I accept the call and put it to my ear. "Hello," I say. Nobody answers me. I look at my phone and see the call is still active. I try again to greet whoever called but hang up when no one responds.

Another scammer. I've been getting a lot lately. I have no time for those tonight, though.

I need to absorb as much information as I can before tomorrow.

I need tomorrow to go well.

Please, go well.

I hope the people I'll manage like me. I hope they aren't nasty. I hope my superiors are easy to work with.

I calm myself again with slow breathing. The president of the company, Nicole Barrett, was so pleasant during the interviews, I remind myself. If the rest of the company is anything like her, tomorrow will be amazing. I hope.

CHAPTER 2

Nicole

How could everything go so wrong, so quickly?

I, of course, know the answer, but would rather not think it.

I was on top of the world, a leader amongst the elite. A role model for women. I was in *Forbes* fucking *Magazine*.

Soon, I'll be nothing.

I look around my home. The comforts of my large luxury apartment in downtown Toronto will mean nothing when I'm behind bars. When I looked down at everyone from my tower, I felt like I was on top of the world.

I sigh. What I would do to have someone to lean on at the moment. Someone who could calm me and tell me everything will be fine.

I don't have that, though. I'm completely alone.

I've been so focused on work that my actual friends abandoned me a long time ago. My colleagues that came up with me as executives

I brought down a long time ago. They were the competition, after all. I had to get ahead of them.

No husband. No children. No time for either of those.

I swirl an expensive cabernet sauvignon in my wine glass, smelling it before taking another sip. I continue to think about all the life decisions that have led me to where I am now.

If my life were a movie, it would easily be as doomed as the *Titanic*. I scowl as I take another sip, tapping the side of the glass with my long nails.

I top my glass, filling it to the brim, nearly finishing the bottle.

I walk out onto the balcony and stare at the shimmering lights in the darkness. I used to be infatuated with the view. I used to be infatuated with my apartment – my life.

I lean over the edge of the balcony and look directly down. I wonder what would happen if I let go of my glass and let it fall, possibly hitting the little specks of people walking below. I laugh and take a long sip.

I'd give up this lifestyle in a heartbeat now, knowing what's in store for me.

Of course, I only see that now when I may face jail time.

Oh, god, what did I do?

I stare at the full moon, taking in a moment of its beauty before screaming into the darkness. With the sounds of the traffic below and the large metropolis, nobody will really hear me anyway, aside from the older couple who lives on the only other apartment on my floor and the few neighbors below me.

I could shout till my head exploded and nobody would care. I look down from my balcony.

Nobody would care if I jumped either.

The thought scares me, and I step back until I'm inside my bedroom. I slam the patio door behind me, taking another long sip.

I look around at the apartment. The expensive artwork, furniture, fireplace. Everything I own is the best.

I'd give it up now if I could.

All I wanted for the last fifteen years was to be where I am today, and now I wish I wasn't here. I wish I wasn't who I am anymore. Hell, I wish I wasn't alive at times, as sad as that is to think.

I walk down the hallway, past my security camera aimed at the front door. Several years ago, there was an armed robber who managed to enter the building and cause some issues for the rich tenants that live here. After that, I decided to get my own system.

It calms me knowing that I'm safe if I have to be.

I walk into a smaller room that I sometimes work out of when I'm not feeling well and stay home, which is rare. I keep all my awards, articles on the wall and anything else that praises me in here.

First I look at the *Forbes Magazine*. "Top woman executives of the year," the article reads. On the cover is me. I take a long drink of wine, squinting at it, not recognizing the confident woman looking back at me.

I sit at my desk. On it is the one picture of me as a child. It was when I spent the summer with my aunt at her farmhouse. My mom thought I'd get a kick out of living amongst the sheep and pigs. She thought it would bother me, but I loved it.

I look at my younger self, my long blond hair tied in pig tails that my aunt Thelma showed me how to do. I'm smiling wide inside the barn with a large pig beside me. I laugh as I remember its name. Gertie the pig.

My smile fades when I think how my aunt Thelma is doing today. She moved to a nursing home recently. She's made me the executor of her will for when she eventually passes, which sadly could be soon. I'll have to figure out what to do with Aunt Thelma's run-down house and old blue barn.

Maybe I'll keep it just for nostalgic reasons.

I wonder if Aunt Thelma is happy with how her life has been. She too has no kids or husband. She only had her farm, and yet she seemed to live a much happier life than I ever could have.

I look at the old picture of me again. What I would do to be that little girl and start over.

I would make different decisions, better

ones. Ones that wouldn't bring me to where I am today.

Maybe I would have gotten married. Had kids. Have a *small* life. Be one of those little specks of people that I always look down at from my balcony.

I was in love, a long time ago. The thought of him upsets me, and I take another sip of wine and put my glass on the desk, for a change letting the alcohol out of my hands tonight.

I open a drawer and take out some paperwork I brought from work the day before.

Tomorrow, we have a new hire starting at Lovely Beauty Supplies. A young woman who I scouted out personally.

Her LinkedIn profile was not bad. She had plenty of management and leadership experience.

She's also married with no children. Her husband is unemployed, most of the time. She was born and raised in Vancouver. I'm sure the move to Toronto, away from her friends and family, will be hard.

Her husband, however, his family lives in Ontario.

They bought a house in a nice area, despite how hideous it is. A fixer upper indeed. It was a place that made my aunt's farmhouse look as luxurious as my apartment.

Alice likes her coffee black, with nothing in it. Some say that's a sign that you're a psychopath, but I disagree since that's how I take mine.

I know her home addresses for the past ten years, her husband's as well.

I know many things about Alice Walker, most of which I learned not from our virtual interview. I hired someone good. A company that I've dealt with before. Their top investigator does fantastic work. When I read their reports, I felt like I knew Alice Walker personally instead of reading words from a piece of paper.

I pick up my wine glass and smile before taking a long drink. I finish the glass and wonder if I should open another bottle.

It's a work night, though. I typically limit myself to two glasses a night, not two bottles.

I look at the candid photos the investigator took of Alice Walker. I take my time looking at the ones he took of her husband, Evan.

From the investigator's reporting, I know him well too now.

Alice is about to start her new executive role at LBS. She's probably nervous right now, in her ugly house, with her handsome husband, anxious for tomorrow to come. I would be. This is the opportunity of a lifetime. If she does well, she'll climb the corporate ladder and make a name for herself.

She could even be the next… Well, me.

I laugh again at the absurdity.

If it wasn't for me finding her profile, she

would have remained in Vancouver. I'm sure she would have done okay for herself, but my company could truly make her.

Too bad for her it won't.

Her first day at work tomorrow is the first day of the last of her dreams.

I walk down the hallway, waving like a silly child to my security camera when I pass it.

If my life is the *Titanic* and I'm going down, I may as well bring a few others with me.

I stand in front of my wine rack and grab the most expensive bottle. I pop the cork aggressively and drink from the bottle.

CHAPTER 3

Alice

I sit in my car, gripping the steering wheel. The parking lot around me is full of activity. People in business attire walk with determination to where they need to go. Instead of joining them, I feel frozen in time, thinking about the mistakes I've made.

This new job has to work out well. I can't even think about what will happen if it doesn't. Not only did we move across the country for this job, but we bought an expensive house in Toronto, one of the world's most inflated real estate markets.

I stare outside at the tall building a few blocks away from me.

Why did I add so much pressure to my life? We should have waited to buy a home until I felt secure in my new job.

I breathe out slowly, trying to calm my quickened pulse. Everything will be okay, I remind myself. If this job doesn't pan out, there will be other work. I can find a good job somewhere else. Sure, it may not pay as well, but we will be fine.

Evan can find work and contribute again.

I breathe out rapidly, my pulse freaking out again. Evan hasn't maintained a job in years. It was something we've fought about on occasion.

I've never understood my husband's attitude towards work. I put in countless hours trying to better myself at my job, while Evan just coasts by, carefree.

I tell myself he just needs to find something he enjoys, and hopefully that happens soon. If my job at LBS goes rotten, I'll need him to do more than renovate the house to continue to afford it.

Moving back to Vancouver isn't what I want to do either. There's nothing there for me now. My mother passed away from cancer several years ago, and my father in the last nine months. I was surprised by how little emotion I had after he finally died. Alzheimer's is a terrible disease that can change the best people into the worst.

My father, David Androise, was anything but good, so Alzheimer's made him unbearable. Ashamed as I am to admit it, I was happier when the disease finally managed to take him.

With my parents both passed, I think about what happens after life ends. I'd like to imagine there's a heaven, and if so I suppose our loved ones are looking down at us.

I like to think my mother is.

If those who passed could see their loved ones, my father would still be more interested in watching a football game from heaven instead.

Stupid girl.

Near the end of his life, that's what he would call me. I cringe thinking of his words as I sit in the car.

When he was lucid, we would talk civilly. When he wasn't, he often thought I was Mom and would ask where his stupid daughter was.

It was a name he called me when he was upset with me as a child. When I did something bad, as children often can, he would call me stupid, and bark at me, scaring me half to death.

One time, when I was eight, I threw a Barbie doll into the air and it struck his scotch glass, causing it to break on the floor. Mom immediately cleaned the mess, and I helped, fearing what my father would do.

"Stupid little girl," he shouted, standing over me as we cleaned. He said I had no respect for money, and that someday I would learn what a penny cost.

For a man who gambled often, and smoked and drank away his disposable income, he had some nerve.

I sit in my car, staring up at the tall tower where I'm about to start my first day at work. Overcoming my fear feels unimaginable.

I breathe out. Do what you always do. Work hard. Follow through with your promises. Work harder. Eventually, you will be seen for what you're worth.

The president of the company hired me directly. She was so pleasant in our interview. She had a caring disposition. A calming aura. She seemed like a wonderful person on camera. It was hard to imagine how today could go bad.

I googled my boss, Nicole Barrett. She was on the cover of *Forbes*. She's what any businesswoman would want to be some day. A true inspiration for what someone can be if they work hard enough.

If I do well with her at this company, who's to say someday I couldn't be on the cover of a magazine myself? I've always been an overachiever.

I could be a president of a company some day.

I can also hear my dad's voice, standing over the top of me as I cleaned his spilt scotch.

Stupid. Little. Girl.

Who did I think I was, trying to be something I wasn't?

I breathe out slowly again.

My worst fear in life is being my parents. I would hate to be a broke, rage-filled person like my father, taking out my inadequacies on my children. Although I loved my mother, I'd hate to be her even more for allowing herself to put up with a man like my father.

We were dirt poor growing up. No matter what, I will never allow myself to have a family if I can't afford one. I won't put a child through what I had, growing up.

I look up at the tall tower again. I got here an hour early, but I've sat in my car in the parking lot for thirty minutes.

The first step is opening the car door, and yet I still feel frozen. I grab my cell phone and call Evan.

Thankfully, he picks up immediately. “Hey, hun.” His voice is so calming and reassuring. I can almost tell he’s smiling as he talks to me. I can imagine his handsome face. Already I start to feel my pulse slow. “Are you settled into your new office? How do you like it?”

“Not yet,” I say and pause.

“Hey Alice!” I hear Tommy, Evan’s brother, call out.

Evan lets him know I said hi back. “Yeah, Tommy just got here,” he says. “We’re doing the demo stuff today.”

“Demo?” I repeat.

“Yeah, it's the fun phase where we basically destroy everything we want to take down in the house so we can start fresh.”

“It’s the best!” Tommy shouts in the background. “It’s where we break shit all day!”

Evan laughs. “Yeah, so it may only be eight in the morning, but we’ve had a few beers already. It’s nice being back in Ontario. I’m glad we came back.”

I know he won't say it, but I’m sure Evan is missing his father right now too. I can imagine the three of them having a beer and breaking the walls of our house together with tools, or hammers, or whatever means of destruction they have in mind today.

"I'm happy that you're happy," I say.

"So, how's work?"

I take a deep breath. "I'm still in the parking lot. I'm sort of freaking out."

He laughs. It's not demeaning. He's heard me and my low moods before. Me freaking out over my insecurities is nothing new.

"You'll be fine," he says reassuringly. "You had your last boss wrapped around your fingers within six months. You'll do even better here."

"That was a small plastic manufacturing company. It's like a mom and pop shop compared to Lovely Beauty Supplies. These guys are the big dogs."

"Hun, you're going to eat these executives' lunches if they don't work nicely with you. You have nothing to worry about. You're perfectly suited for this job. You're going to do fantastic. And... worse case, you find a new one. Screw 'em."

I'd hate to tell him how hard that could be, so I don't bother explaining it now. I would love to have his black and white thinking cap on all the time. That's something I can't do. I see the big picture. If it doesn't work out here, how can I get another executive job somewhere else? If I have a blank spot in my resume, that will raise questions in future interviews. Finding a good management job in Toronto isn't as easy as my husband likes to think. Since he's never worked for a company longer than a few years, he doesn't understand.

"Besides," Evan continues, "you said your boss was really nice."

"Nicole," I say. "Yeah, she seemed great."

"So," he says enthusiastically, "why are you so worried? You're a great judge of people. After all, you married me." Tommy laughs hard in the background while making a loud thud. I can only imagine he's breaking something with a heavy tool at the moment and worry if these men know what they're doing. "Shut up!" Evan shouts to his brother. "What I'm saying is, you a'ready know you have a half-decent boss. That's half the battle. I'm sure your new coworkers will be fine too. Now, do me a favor."

He waits for me to ask. "What's the favour?" I say.

"Hang up the phone," he says, "and open the car door. Go to work, and I love you."

I smile. "I love you too. Have fun breaking the house."

"Oh, we will."

I end the call, and as he asked, open the car door. The look of fear in my face suddenly vanishes as I put on my executive face. It's almost as if I'm an actress staring at a mirror, getting into character. I straighten my pants suit before grabbing my suitcase.

I look up at the intimidating tower a few blocks away, hiding my fear. I pay for parking before leaving the lot and hurry across the street with the other businessmen and women. I become one of them as I walk with determination to the high tower in front of me.

When I enter, I quickly look at the building directory. I already know the main office of LBS is on the thirtieth floor, but check anyway. Knowing where I'm going has a way of calming me.

Several businessmen get off at their floors one by one, until it's my turn. I take a deep breath, concealing my worries, as I take the first step onto the floor of my new job. The large signage on the wall says: "Lovely Beauty Supplies. Have a Beautiful Day."

I walk down the corridor as several men pass in the other direction. They don't notice me, but I nod and greet them a good morning. One of the men gives a small smile back while the other ignores me.

At the end of the narrow hallway, the space opens to a large area full of half cubicles with busy people on the phone inside them. The office is buzzing with customer service reps talking to people. Large offices with glass walls surround the outer borders of the cubicle area, all with panoramic windows facing downtown Toronto.

It's almost overwhelming. I have never worked in a tall business tower like this before. The last building I worked at had only three floors.

"Can I help you, Ms.?" a friendly voice asks. I turn and a receptionist at a large desk beams at me. She's a petite woman, her make-up applied perfectly, which makes sense for a young woman working for a leading beauty supply company. It's not caked on, and looks natural, bringing out her youthful appearance and bright blue eyes. Her long blond hair casts a soft glow that compliments her complexion.

"Yes, hi," I say, matching her smile. "I'm Alice Walker, the new..."

"Yes, the new executive of sales. Welcome to Lovely Beauty Supplies. Nicole told me to expect you. She asked that you go to her office when you arrive."

I look around the office area and the many faces in the room. "I'm sorry, which office is hers?"

"Ms. Barrett's office is the largest one, at the northeast of the building."

I look around the room again, feeling completely stupid. "Sorry, which direction is that?"

The receptionist stands up and points behind me. "No problem, Ms. Walker. Ms. Barrett's office is that one." I turn and see her office. Somehow I managed to not spot the obviously massive office directly behind me.

"Thank you, and please, call me Alice," I say. "I'm not one for formalities. And your name again was?"

"Thanks, Alice," she says. "I'm Leigh Olson, Nicole's executive assistant. I'll let Ms. Barrett know you're here."

I thank Leigh again before turning towards the office.

"Have a beautiful morning," Leigh says. I turn back to her, surprised, and she gives a thin smile. "They make me say that," she whispers, giving a grin back. "But honestly, have a great first day."

I thank her again and head towards Nicole Barrett's office. I can see inside it from the outside as I get closer. Actually, I can see inside everyone's office around here. No one has any privacy. At any time, your coworkers can see what you're doing, or not doing, when at work. The thought is intimidating, but I try not to think of it.

Nicole looks as pretty as she had in the virtual meeting. A slim figure with long, straight, blond hair. A sharp smile.

She's speaking to an older woman with red hair. The other woman's head is tilted towards the floor. Nicole reaches across the desk and pats the woman's hand. It comes off as endearing, until I see the older woman stand up quickly and rush to the door.

The other woman nearly bursts out of the office, her eyes watering, nose sniffling. She quickly brushes past me, nearly knocking me over. Beside Leigh the receptionist, two security guards have magically appeared out of thin air.

The older woman with red hair stops and one of them asks her to please not make a scene. She snaps loudly, "I'm vice president of this company! You can't just kick me out onto the street!"

"Don't make a scene," the guard says again. He touches her arm gently and the woman brushes him off, storming down the hall, the sounds of sniffles dying away down the narrow hallway.

The busy office suddenly appears to still as everyone watches. It's as if someone hit the pause button as everyone watched the woman leave. Even the receptionist seems startled as she looks back at me and gives a thin smile.

At the bottom of her desk, large lettering reads: "Have A Beautiful Day."

"You must be Alice," a strong voice says behind me. I turn and Nicole Barrett is grinning at me. The smile is nearly identical to the one she shared with the woman who was just terminated. Someone must have hit the play button again as the office is suddenly back to being busy now that Nicole is outside her office.

I look back at her, attempting to hide my fear of what I just witnessed. I quickly managed to put out my hand. "Alice Walker. Nice to meet you in person."

Nicole Barrett smiles at me. "Please, come inside my office."

CHAPTER 4

Nicole sits comfortably behind her desk, and I sit opposite, trying to match her confidence as I look back, but the image of the woman crying and storming out of the office with security beside her is hard to ignore.

I'm surprised by how youthful Nicole looks in person as well, and wonder if she uses her own beauty supply products herself. She has long blond hair and light blue eyes, just like the receptionist. Leigh could almost be her much younger sister, except her aura was much more welcoming. I'm not sure how I feel being around Nicole.

My new boss continues to smile at me. I must be squirming in my chair. It starts to get awkward as I know one of us should say something, but I'm still in shock.

I finally muster the courage to find words. "Thank you for—"

Nicole interrupts me, speaking confidently over me. "I'm so sorry, Alice, that you had to witness that. It wasn't my intention for you to see. Unfortunately, our vice president hasn't been working out for some time now. We here at LBS like to give employees the best support we can, but if they're not putting in their side of what's expected, eventually we have to end our relationship. We feel it's mutually beneficial for us if something isn't working out." She pauses.

"Yes, I understand. That must have been difficult for both of you," I say, keeping a business demeanour. Firing people isn't something I've enjoyed when I've had to. Even when I felt completely justified in my decision to terminate someone's employment, I hated seeing their face when I told them. It was human nature.

"Not really," Nicole says, maintaining her smile. "She knew this was going to happen, and it was time for her to leave." She waits for me to respond, but I stare blankly at her. "So, how are you settling in Toronto? Being from Vancouver, a large city, this must not be too intimidating."

"I love it here already, thank you. Your office is certainly something else. I'm incredibly grateful for the opportunity to work with Lovely Beauty Supplies. Again, thank you for not only hiring me, but believing in the work I can contribute to this company." I smile back confidently.

That was nice, I think. Not too arrogant. Confident in what I said, but with an understanding that not only I will benefit from working with them, but they will benefit from my work. A well put together response.

"Right," Nicole says curtly. "Anyway, I believe in our last correspondence you mentioned you were struggling to find a place to rent. Did you situate yourself okay?"

"Yes, thank you," I say, a bit put off by her response. I almost feel like the large office is getting smaller with each moment. "We're living in the West Hill area. It's nice. We actually bought a house there too. It's a bit of a fixer upper, though."

Overshare of information. I'm waiting for Nicole to give me an awkward look or a quick reply. Instead, she smiles. "Well, that's wonderful. I used to live in that area when I first moved into Toronto. Small world." Nicole laughs. "So, is your husband a handy kind of man? I hope so with your new house; it sounds like it needs some work done."

"He does okay." I laugh. "Him and his brother are demolishing parts we want to renovate. Hopefully I won't come home tonight to find the house broken in half."

"Do you two have any children?"

"No, we don't. Evan would really love to have one someday soon, but I'm very career focused." I catch myself thinking what Nicole must be thinking. She hires a new woman and already she's talking about a not too distant maternity leave. It's the last thing she would want. "I have plenty of child-rearing years left," I say with a laugh. "Right now, I'm focused on my work."

"That's wonderful to hear," she says. "Are

you and your husband… happy?"

That's an odd question. I've never had a superior or even a co-worker ask me something like that before.

"Uh, yes, very. He's a good man."

"And… very handy. All good things. I'm very happy for you."

"Thanks, Ms. Barrett."

"Nicole, please. Please call me Nicole."

I smile. "Thanks. "

"I'm happy you're a part of the LBS now as well."

I fidget in my seat a bit when she says it. It's something I wondered about for some time, even before our first interview.

"Can I ask you a question, Nicole?"

"Of course," she says, giving me her confident smile back and leaning in with her full attention.

"Why did you reach out to me? You scouted me out for the interview we had."

"My executive assistant, Leigh, I believe you met her when you first entered the office. I asked her to find me some suitable candidates for the position. I wanted to specifically find someone who was from out of the city. New blood, I guess. I've worked with many of the executive salesmen and women out here. I wanted to work with someone fresh, new. Unfortunately, we've been having some struggles at LBS. I saw the work you did with your last employer. Your time there matched their surge in sales. I knew Leigh had done great work in finding you. Leigh is only temporarily working at the front counter. Unfortunately our other receptionist is off on maternity leave and we're in the process of hiring. I'm glad you mentioned you don't plan on leaving me anytime soon either. I love little humans as well, but I need to keep my best executives with me right now."

Nicole stands up abruptly, and I quickly do the same. "Well, I think it's time for us to do a little tour now." Nicole starts off by bringing me back to Leigh and introducing us more officially this time.

Leigh welcomes me again, and I grin back. She appears to be a nice woman. Organized. She was part of the reason I was hired, apparently, so I like her even more now.

Nicole walks me around the cubicle area and introduces me to several supervisors of different departments. I take my time to greet each one and try my best to take a mental note of something unique about their appearance and try and match it to their name. It's a trick I learned to remember people.

Remembering people's names is so important, especially if you're management. These supervisors and the people who work under them will need to learn to trust me, and building a strong rapport initially can be so important. Letting them know that you remembered their name after meeting a building full of people can start that connection the proper way.

I'm impressed by how well Nicole knows her staff as well. She must have taken the same leadership courses I have, or maybe being one is just natural for her. I've worked for companies where the higher-ups had no clue who any of the underlings were. Not only did Nicole know every supervisor's name by heart, but even customer service reps. Everyone greeted her warmly, and she did the same.

Even Nicole showing me around personally was something that astounded me. She could have easily made Leigh do it, but she wanted to be a part of this on-boarding process. Already I felt a strong rapport building with Nicole despite what happened with the vice president being fired on the day I arrived at the office.

Nicole continues to show me the break room, and more impressively, an outdoor patio. I feel light-headed when I look all the way down from the rail. Nicole jokes about not coming outside on a windy day. I've always had a fear of heights and likely won't be coming out here anytime soon.

Lastly, Nicole stands in front of a large, empty office. Unlike the many others surrounding the cubicle area, this one has no one sitting inside. After Nicole's office, it appears to be the second largest here.

"And," Nicole said with a warm smile, "last but not least, your office." She opens the glass door, and waves for me to enter.

I slowly step inside, and my mouth nearly hits the floor.

This is my office now? How did I ever manage this? Am I even good enough to deserve an office like this?

For a moment I feel my insecurities start to clamour inside me, feeling inferior to this room I'll be working in every day. I grew up in a one-bedroom house, with no space to call my own. I slept on the couch in the living room.

Now, as an adult, I stand thirty floors up in a tower, an executive at a leading beauty supply company. And this is my office.

I look around the glass walls, and watch all the staff working hard in their cubicles. Just like when I was a kid, I still don't exactly have privacy, but I've made it. This is a dream come true.

"Is it to your liking?" Nicole asks.

I feel a tear welling in my eye and don't want the president of the company to see how emotional this moment is for me. I casually wipe my eyes.

"This is beautiful, thank you so much, and for the tour as well." When I'm confident my eyes are more dry, I turn to her. "I really am having a beautiful day." I nearly laugh at my pun of the business motto.

Nicole gives a thin smile. "So, this was

actually the vice president's office. She was the woman who was let go today. This office will be for the future vice president, but since we are lacking office space at the moment, I thought it would be great for you to have this spot. Or, who knows, maybe this could be your permanent office some day." She smiles again and pats my hand. "I'm happy you're here, Alice. Welcome to the team."

I thank her again before she leaves. As Nicole exits through the glass door, her expression quickly vanishes, replaced by something like a scowl.

For a moment, it's off-putting. Some of the most amazing people I've worked with have the same face though. I know they have a lot on their mind. I wonder at times if I do the same. All these executives have so much on their mind every day.

Nicole Barrett is the same of course, but much more. President of a large company, and today she had to let go of her vice president. That position won't be easy to replace.

She must have much more than usual on her mind today. A new hire, and a high-level termination.

I let her words sink in for a moment. She joked about this being my permanent office. Well, that must have been a joke, right? She couldn't really mean it.

She must not be too impressed with the other executives here if I'm even remotely in consideration. That means that if I put in the time and hard work, it's a possibility that I could get the job.

The first day's going even better than I expected. I drop my briefcase on my long wood desk and stare out the broad windows at the city of Toronto.

I smile again, thinking I must be living someone else's life.

If only my mother could see her little girl now. Besides staying with my father, my mom was smart. She could have made something for herself in this world. Instead, she let my father put limits on how far she could go, which was to mostly to the kitchen and maybe a weekly trip to the grocery store.

She was to be a wife who kept the house clean and prepared the meals each day. She was forbidden to work. That was a man's job. Despite my father struggling with providing for his family, he wouldn't let her get a job.

I feel my father's words in my mind.

Stupid. Little. Girl.

I take a deep breath. My father couldn't be any more wrong. Look at what I've accomplished so far. If I do well in the next few months here at LBS, then I could climb even higher.

I sit at my desk, taking in the people working busily outside the room. I know I need to stop being a tourist here and start doing the same. Already a stack of paperwork is on my desk waiting for my review.

There's a lot of work for me to do today, even with it being my first day. A big meeting is scheduled where not only am I to be introduced but I'm expected to be an active participant. A breakdown of what we'll be reviewing at the meeting was on my desk. I want to do some research beforehand to be prepared to contribute efficiently.

Before I start working, I open my briefcase, and take out a picture frame of me and Evan on our honeymoon in the Dominican Republic.

I smile, reminiscing of the day it was taken.

Even though I hate how unmotivated he can be, he has supported me every step in my journey. Not many professional women have that in a partner. A man like my father certainly wouldn't have.

That's why I married Evan, though.

I shouldn't only celebrate what I've done to be here today in an office like this, but I need to celebrate my husband as well for his support.

We did this together.

My phone vibrates and out of habit I take it out and answer it. "Hello?" I immediately regret answering my phone at work as I see Nicole walking into the office beside mine. She could easily see me taking a personal call on my first day.

I'm about to hang up when I hear heavy breathing on the other end.

"Hello?" I repeat. Through the glass walls I see Nicole sit at her desk, and I turn in my chair and quickly end the call. I put my cell phone in my briefcase. Now's not time for interruptions or taking calls.

Now it's time for me to show Nicole and everyone at LBS that I'm good at what I do.

CHAPTER 5

I sit in my living room, decompressing with a glass of wine. Making first impressions is exhausting, but I think I did quite well.

The team meeting where I was introduced to all the supervisors and other executives went swimmingly. Not only did I manage to remember most of the people I had met earlier that day, but I even contributed well to the meeting.

A very productive day.

By the end of the day, Leigh had posted for the position of vice president. I stared at the job advertisement, wondering what kind of a chance I'd have at that position.

At the meeting, I felt there were a few candidates who came off confident in their jobs. For a top-tier company, I was surprised how friendly everyone was. I assumed it was going to be more cutthroat. I assumed Nicole would be tough after what I saw with the former vice president as well, but she was the friendliest of the bunch.

She came by my office several times to check on how my first day was going. Each time we made small talk, which also went well. I'm sociable but find it hard to continue to come up with continuous things to talk about throughout the day when I don't know someone well.

I hear the sound of a sledgehammer striking drywall from the basement, followed by Tommy and Evan laughing.

My new house, if you can call it that, is in a shambles. I didn't expect them to gut nearly the entire basement.

Our new place will be a dream home, he promises me.

We sometimes watch home renovation shows to relax at night. While we snack, Evan always comments on how he would handle the reno we're watching. His input makes sense, even though I have no clue what I'm listening to, so I suppose I trust him with his work. He's done a lot of renovations before in our last house, but those were much smaller jobs than renovating nearly the whole building.

He showed me the estimates for what we would be saving by having him do the work instead of hiring a company and I was on board.

I hear the swing of the sledgehammer, followed by something being destroyed, followed by the giggling of grown men.

I don't remember the reno guys in the show getting drunk and breaking everything but I'm hoping for a dream reveal like at the end of the programs.

Evan comes up the stairs and grins at me.

"I think we're having a bit too much fun down there," he says, finishing a beer. He starts to walk towards the kitchen.

"I think you two need to be cut off." I laugh. "No more boozing on the job."

"I was actually grabbing a water," Evan says, but opens the fridge to get another beer. "Tommy, on the other hand, continues to have fun. We may need to give him a ride home."

"Oh, brother," I say.

"Exactly," he says, laughing. Evan sits on the couch beside me and pats my thighs. "We didn't get a chance to talk about your first day."

"It went well... everything. The people are nice. There's this receptionist who I thought was really great. Actually, she's my boss's executive assistant. She's just very sociable. She asked me out for coffee tomorrow. Nicole, my new boss, told me that Leigh was part of the reason I was hired in the first place. She was the one who found my profile on LinkedIn."

"So I guess you're buying the coffee tomorrow." Evan laughs.

"We had this large meeting. I remembered people's names and they remembered mine. Then there's even... I don't know, even a chance for a promotion."

"Already?"

"Well, yeah. This woman was fired today, and apparently, she was the vice president."

"On your first day at the job someone was fired?" Evan says, uninspired.

"Yeah, it was off-putting, but I don't know the background. I'm sure there's a good reason."

Evan nods. "I guess, but that has me worried." He strokes my thigh again and stands up. "I have to pee," he says romantically.

"Okay, well, you take care of that," I say, shaking my head. I watch as my husband gets off the couch and saunters to the bathroom, which is one of the few rooms the brothers have not completely destroyed. He's wearing his light-colored jeans and black tank top. His clothes are dirtied and his skin is glistening with sweat that makes his lean muscles look tighter.

If his brother wasn't downstairs, I'd be making him take a much longer break from his renovation work. I take another sip of my wine, reflecting on how handsome my husband is.

As I think about what I want to do with him tonight, my phone rings, breaking my concentration. I quickly picked it up and notice it's from an unknown number.

"Hello, Alice speaking," I answer.

"Hello, who is this?" Silence answers me.

I look at my phone and see the call is still connected. Suddenly I start to hear breathing. It's faint but there.

"Who is this?" I ask. "Why are you calling?"

The call ends, just in time for Evan to come out from the bathroom. Tommy walks up the stairs. He grins at me as he places his phone in his pants pocket. He's wearing no shirt and, like his brother, has put good effort into maintaining a muscled physique. Evan is easily the more handsome brother. Tommy is definitely known for being more, well, let's call it silly. Despite that, Tommy's held his teaching job for some time now and makes a good income.

"Where's my beer?" he asks.

Evan tosses it to him across the room. "Here. Bar is now closed."

"We're just getting started," Tommy says, opening it and taking a long sip. "I'm off for the summer now and we have a lot of work to do."

"Thanks again," I say to him.

"No sweat," he says. "Besides if I let Evan do this on his own, he'll screw it up like he does everything."

"Shut up," Evan jokes back. "It's nearly nine, though; we should pick up where we left off tomorrow. I don't want to piss off the new neighbors with all the racket."

"Fine, fine," Tommy says, taking another drink.

"How was the school year for you?" I ask. I quickly glance at Evan to make sure I haven't upset him by asking his brother. I know how much Evan hates hearing his brother talk about a career he once had aspirations for.

"It was great," Tommy said. "Another solid year. Since I became a PE teacher, life has honestly been so much, well, easier. No more lesson planning, besides choosing if the kiddos are going to play dodgeball or basketball today. I'm still at the same grad school. Love what I do." Tommy quickly glances at Evan as well, who remains quiet.

"Happy for you, Tommy," I say. I stand and raise my glass to him.

"Tell her about your girlfriend," Evan says, chiming into the conversation.

Tommy scoffs. "I wouldn't say *girlfriend* per se."

"Tommy Walker," I say playfully. "Has an actual woman managed to capture your heart?"

"He's basically married, he tells me." Evan laughs. "We should expect invitations to double dates soon enough."

Tommy shakes his head. "No, no, no. I don't know about any of that. It's still too early to tell where it's going. We're not, like, official. How do you even know if you're official anyways at our age?"

"You ask them," I answer in a deadpan voice. Evan nearly spits out his water. "You know that thing called a conversation? You have one of those and ask."

Tommy laughs. "Yeah, maybe that's why I'm

still single."

"Well, tell us about her," I ask. I always love hearing about Tommy's dating life. The bad luck he has with women is a running joke.

"Not this time," Tommy says.

"Well, give us a name at least," I demand.

Tommy shakes his head. "Not a peep from me. I always tell you about my dating life and it doesn't work out. I want this one to work out, I do. I feel I'll jinx it if I say a word. Maybe soon I'll have one of those things – what did you call it? – a conversation, and figure it out, and—" He smiles at me. "—I'll let you know how it goes."

"Fair enough," I say, clinking my wine glass to his beer can.

"So, how'd the new job go today?" Tommy asks.

I repeat to him what I told Evan, and he nods. "Happy for you, too," he says. We clink our beer and wine glass again.

"And soon enough she'll be vice president!" Evan says.

Tommy looks at me. "Already?"

"No!" I shout. "Not at all. Evan's messing with me. There's just an opening for the job. I won't get it, I'm sure."

"Some woman got canned today," Evan says.

"That's too bad," Tommy says. "Well, maybe not bad for you though. Is your new boss decent?"

"Nicole," I say, nodding. "Yeah, she's been

great." I think about the security guard escorting the former vice president out of the building and the anger she had. The tears falling from her face as she left.

Well, I hope Nicole's great.

Tommy takes a long sip and finishes his can of beer. "So, who's giving me a ride home?"

CHAPTER 6

Nicole

I'm at the office late at night. It's not unusual for me to be here at this time, long after everyone has left for the day. It's gotten to the point where security knows that if lights on the floor are on, it will be me they see in the office. They thankfully don't disturb me.

Tonight, though, I've been doing anything but work.

All I can do is sit in the office and wonder what will happen next.

My entire career is about to implode. I'm just waiting to see the fuse so I know when the explosion will happen.

It could happen any day now. I walk around the empty cubicles and look at the items my workers have pinned on their walls. Most have pictures of family and loved ones inside their work areas.

My office is bare except for the expensive artwork littering the one wall that's not made of glass.

I walk back to my office and stare out into the dark Toronto sky. I look down at the busy cars at the intersection below. I can hear the faint sounds of traffic.

I scowl, thinking how enraged I am.

What if I made better decisions?

What if I focused on filling my walls with memories of loved ones, even children? I never wanted the pesky things, but now that I'm over thirty, I have regrets.

Every time I stare down from up high, I think about how freeing it would be if I jumped. Would I even be scared if I plummeted to my death? Part of me imagines I would discover I had wings and fly away to a different life, one I actually want to keep living in.

Instead, I'm stuck with mine, and the consequences that are coming.

I need wine.

Today wasn't so bad though. Firing my vice president was fun. Some people get uncomfortable when having to terminate someone, but not me. For most, they deserve it. They're actions brought them to their destiny of sitting in front of me as I told them those two terrifying words.

'You're fired.'

It's their own reasons that brought them there. My former vice president was no different. Well, a little I suppose. She started digging around too much into what I was doing. She could have discovered what I've done. She would be more than happy to take my place as president. So now she has no job.

That's what you get when you mess with me. I would wish her well in finding a new job, but that will be nearly impossible for her to do it in this province. She may even need to move continents to find work.

Her name is garbage because I said that's what she is. Other companies won't want to hire someone like her after what I did to her reputation.

She's ruined, and I'm not, at least for now.

Alice Walker's first day went well, I'm sure she imagined. She must be at home, fluttering about her perfect life, happy as can be. I gave her a whiff of that vice president position and she perked up fast.

She actually thinks she has a shot.

I know she's a few years younger than me. Naivety is something for the young that can be cured by age.

Alice Walker may not find that out until it's too late for her.

I walk over to her office and open the door. I take my time, standing over her desk before sitting in her chair. Her work area is tidy, as I expected. Paperwork neatly piled on her desk.

A picture of her and her husband, Evan, stares at me. Their happy faces disgust me. What a lovely moment they shared when it was taken. I imagine soon enough her walls will be decorated with other loving memories she will make. Many more with Evan.

Despite what she told me today, soon enough she'll have kids too. Her life will be full of happy times.

Maybe there's something I can do about that part.

I pick up the picture of the happy couple and stare at it, taking my time to see how handsome Evan Walker has become.

I remember what he did and crash the picture frame onto the desk. Glass flies across the surface and onto the floor.

When I raise my hand, there's a small cut on my palm. I suck at the blood, staining my hand with my lipstick.

Our new no-mess lipstick brand does not appear to be living up to its promise. I suck on my wound as I stand up from the desk and leave the office.

CHAPTER 7

Alice

I take my time stepping over the broken glass on my office carpet. I pick up the broken picture frame with two fingers barely touching it. Evan's pearly white teeth shine through the smashed glass. I place it back down on the desk gently, wondering—

"What happened?" a voice says from behind me. I turn and Nicole is staring at me intensely. "Don't touch the glass. Try not to get hurt." She laughs. "Don't want a workplace injury your first week."

"I'm sorry," I say, "I'm not sure what happened here. I came into my office and the picture frame was broken."

"Midnight cleaner," Nicole says confidently. "Mark something, I think his name is. I always see him late at night cleaning with his headphones on. He must have banged into the desk or something and didn't hear." She points at the mess. "Was that an expensive frame?"

"No, not at all," I say. "Sorry about this.

Where can I get a broom or vacuum?"

"Not your fault at all, Alice, don't worry. I'll request a cleaner to come to your office right away. One with no headphones on so there's no more damage." She laughs at her own joke. "Maybe don't sit at your desk until they come, though."

"No problem," I say with a smile. "Thanks. That meeting today, it's at ten, right?"

"That's right. How did you feel about your first meeting yesterday?"

"I think I contributed well. You have a great team of people here."

"I do. I like to think I hire the best. Maybe just not the best cleaners. Speaking of cleaning…" She puts a finger to her chin. "If I remember you live in the West Hill area, right?"

"Good memory. That's right."

"They have the best dry cleaning place in the city just a few minutes from you," she says with a smile. "I really recommend them. Would it be okay if you pick up mine tomorrow for me? They open very early so you won't be late. It's such a hassle with me being downtown." She watches me for a response.

I take a moment to collect my thoughts. Is she seriously asking me to pick up her dry cleaning? I've never had a boss ask me to do something so meaningless. Yesterday she's hinting at a promotion and today I've been demoted to completing her small tasks.

Does Nicole ask all her staff to do trivial things for her? I hate to sound like that kind of person, but isn't this more the duty of an executive assistant like Leigh?

"No problem," I answer, trying not to let my annoyance show.

"You really are a lifesaver," Nicole says, her smile widening. "I'll drop by with the ticket you need to pick it up. Thanks!" She abruptly leaves the office and I watch her through the glass as she turns and walks into her own.

I lower my head and wonder if I'm overthinking this. Do all her staff do little things for Nicole to make her life a little easier? If she was a friend who asked me to pick up something for her near my house, I'd likely do it for them.

I don't know Nicole well, though, and she's my superior.

Glass breaks under my foot as I take another step. Mark the cleaner must have really banged into the table hard.

I walk back to my desk and take a look at my planner. I see that the meeting today is at nine thirty, not ten.

Seems odd as well that someone like Nicole wouldn't have realized that. She seems so on top of everything she does. Maybe there's a meeting with other management members before Nicole joins in at ten? At some of the other places I worked, the top executives wouldn't be there for an entire meeting.

I'm glad I checked my planner. I would have been very late for my second meeting.

I see movement outside my office, with Leigh and an older man with white combed over hair smiling at me.

"Good morning, Alice," Leigh says. "I heard there's been a little accident that needed tending to." She grins. "Steve is here to help."

I nod at the cleaner. "Thanks so much, Steve."

"No problem," he says.

"Sorry," I say, "is there any way you can take the picture out of the frame? I just want to keep the picture."

Steve stares at me and for a moment I realize I'm asking something of this man that I could have done on my own and feel silly. He must feel exactly how I just did when Nicole asked me to do something not in my job description.

"I'm sorry, Steve. Never mind, I'll grab it myself."

"Please, no," Steve says, putting up a hand. "I'll take care of everything. Not a problem. Just give me fifteen minutes or so to clean up here." He looks at Leigh. "I should grab the vacuum though." He nods at her before leaving back down the hall.

"How's your morning going?" I ask Leigh.

"Good. Always busy around here. Always something that needs to be done. Thankfully, it's my coffee break."

"That sounds wonderful," I say.

"Well, Steve is going to need some time here. Come with me. There's this nice coffee place on the main floor."

"You sure?"

"Yeah, it beats watching Steve clean. Besides, once you have a sip, you'll hate me for it. You'll be spending a lot of money there afterwards."

I leave with Leigh and as we walk down the hall, I notice Nicole at her desk watching us. I quickly look away but can almost feel her gaze at my back and feel uncomfortable.

Leigh and I make small talk on the elevator until we're on the main floor. I step into the coffee shop and a wave of aromatic bliss washes over me. The air is thick and rich with the smell of freshly roasted coffee beans. Leigh orders a medium mocha, and I get a large coffee.

We sit at a small table facing a window. I take a moment to watch all the bustling people outside. Many are in their business wear.

"So how's day two?" Leigh asks, taking a sip and wincing. "Too hot."

"Well LBS seems like a great place to work. Friendly staff," I say, smiling at her. "Ones that will take you out for coffee and show you around. I really do appreciate you helping me get settled in." I take a sip of my coffee. "Mmm," I say, making a genuine face of yumminess. "That's really great."

"Dare I say better than Starbucks." She

laughs. "And no problem. Besides some day I may need to ask you for a raise and I'll make sure to mention, 'Remember that time I took you out for coffee?'"

I laugh. "Well, you should have paid for mine then." We both laugh. "I'm just joking, of course," I quickly add in case my veil of professionalism has disappeared. "But really, I do appreciate the help. Nicole seems really nice."

Leigh gives a thin smile and sips her coffee again. "That handsome man in the picture frame that was destroyed I guess is your husband?"

"Evan, and yeah. Our anniversary is next week. Two years."

"Ugh. That's my 'I'm happy for you' sound but not for myself. I need a man." She looks outside the window at the people walking by. "Look at all of them. They may be wearing three-piece suits, but many are just little boys in fancy clothes."

I laugh. "You would have loved the company I worked for before here. A few eligible rich bachelors there, but they were the worst. They knew they were rich and attractive and showed it."

"That would have been terrible, but I would have cried myself to sleep while he paid for my Porsche if it worked out."

I grin at her joke. It's too bad she's not a manager or another executive. Being in a new city is hard, especially if you don't know anybody. Would it be wrong to cultivate a friendship with someone I have a direct leadership role over, though?

“You're such a pretty young woman,” I say. “Boys in suits must be lined up.”

She makes another sound of disappointment. “I do okay, but let's just say I have problems choosing the right ones. I like really crappy men, apparently.”

“How long have you been at LBS?”

“Six years now,” she says, taking a long sip. “Have a Beautiful Day,” she mocks. “I’m good at my job and delivering whatever message Nicole wants me to convey, but I would be okay if that saying died and I could just say bye like a normal person.”

I laugh again. I’m surprised at how professional Leigh was over the phone and now how candid she is talking to me. I would be intimidated talking to an executive so freely. I suppose it may be because I’m new, or maybe she senses that I have a fun side as well.

I only just met Leigh, but I would hire her for my own executive assistant in a minute.

“So how is working for Nicole?” I ask.

She takes a very long sip before finding the right words. “Well, she’s been great to me. I've gained her trust along the way. Let’s just say she’s fair. She can be hard, but in my opinion, the people who don't like her are upset with their own insecurities. I mean, if you work hard, do what's expected, or even better, go above and beyond, you will get on splendidly with her. I can already tell you'll do great here."

I smile. Those are all qualities that I have. Leigh must sense that given that it was her who found my profile on LinkedIn.

"Thanks again, for everything that you've done."

Leigh takes another sip. "Well, I guess you'll be an easy executive to please if it only takes a cup of coffee."

I raise my cup to her. "Only if it's an exceptional cup of coffee."

Leigh grins and takes her final sip. "You'll do great things here. Just don't ever get on Nicole's bad side."

After our coffee date, we go back to the thirtieth floor. Leigh is back at her reception counter. I walk past Nicole's office but she's not there. I'm thankful. I almost feel like she's a hawk watching me. I was worried about catching her gaze when I scurried back to my office.

When I step inside my own, I'm relieved that my desk and carpet are clean. I can finally get some work done today.

I'm upset, though, when the picture of my husband and I is nowhere in sight.

CHAPTER 8

I settle into my office, trying to get myself mentally prepared for the meeting that will take place soon. This is my first week, after all. Now is my time to make a solid good impression. I can't slack. I can't be average.

I need to stand out, especially since Nicole mentioned the promotion.

It's hard to do any of that when I'm pissed off wondering where the hell the picture of my husband and I went. The cleaner, Steve, said he would leave it for me.

Perhaps he did and he's keeping it in his office, although that would make no sense.

The idea of something so personal of mine not being where I want it bothers me. He likely threw it away.

Having Evan watch me as I worked made me feel like he was in the room with me. As annoyed as I can be with his lack of care for employment, his carefree attitude has a way of rubbing off on me, especially when I see him.

If something doesn't work out in life, he just

moves on. No fuss, well, a little. He has his temper. He will get upset for a little while. After a short burst of anger, he drops it and thinks of what he'll do next, or sometimes, do nothing.

I feel I never had that luxury in life. I was always trying to figure out how to be the best, how I could be the top of the class in school. How could I be the best on the volleyball team? How could I be better?

Evan doesn't care about any of those things.

Sometimes it amazes me that a man like him and a woman like me ever fell in love.

Opposites attract, I suppose.

Having Evan in my office made me feel like no matter what, everything will be okay.

Now he's gone.

How the hell do I even print a new picture?

The photo and frame was a gift from Evan a few years ago. I don't think I've had to print off a picture in over a decade. Most of my memories are all digital or ordered online.

Ugh. I could scream at Steve. I don't want to be that kind of executive, though. I want to be the type that workers feel is approachable. I want to be likable, even if I'm their superior. Yelling at the custodian won't help.

I work through my frustration in preparation for the meeting. That's when I see movement outside the offices. I spot several managers and other high-ranking management come out from the meeting room. Last to leave is Nicole.

I look at the time to confirm I'm not crazy. I stare at my calendar again. The meeting is supposed to be at nine thirty, so why is everyone leaving?

I get my answer soon enough when Nicole opens my door. She has a weary smile. "Hey, where were you?" she asks, getting to the point.

"Did the meeting time get moved? I thought it was at nine thirty."

"It was, but I needed to move it for another meeting I have today," she says. "I even came to your office, but you weren't here."

"While the cleaner was taking care of my office, I grabbed coffee."

"I looked in the kitchen too but didn't see you there," she says, waiting for a better answer.

"Well, I went to that coffee place on the main floor. I thought—"

Nicole takes a deep breath. "Sorry, I guess I didn't realize you would take such a long break so early in the morning. I was hoping you would be at that meeting. It's okay. I would give you the notes from the meeting, but Leigh wasn't there either to take them."

I exhale slowly, trying to catch my breath. "She was actually with me, sorry. I didn't realize the meeting was going to be moved. Next time I will wait to confirm my day before splurging on fancy coffee." I smile but Nicole doesn't.

"Please do," she says. "I'll have to talk to Leigh too." She looks outside at the reception area. Leigh is speaking on the phone, smiling. Nicole looks back at me and her face lightens. "It's okay. I have your personal number. I know we're waiting for your corporate cell to come but next time I'll call you on your own to avoid this again."

I agree and Nicole leaves my office without saying another word. I sit in my chair and suddenly feel like I'm shrinking. It's almost like the natural sunlight from outside and from the surrounding offices is magnifying the heat and lasering on me. I could melt on the spot.

Now would be the time that I would look at Evan's handsome face for comfort. I try to find confidence in myself.

"Everything is going to be okay," I whisper. I type on my laptop aimlessly at some of the product supplies on the company's website. I have no purpose at the moment besides trying to calm myself.

Everything is not okay. I screwed up big time. My second day and I'm already truant from an important meeting.

Nicole didn't even verbally tell me what happened at it.

What president wants to go over important details shared at a meeting? None. They want their management to be there, in person, attentively listening to what's being said. They don't want them getting coffee with the receptionist.

I wonder how much trouble I got Leigh into. I stare outside my office and she's on the phone still. I stare at the bold letters of our company's motto below her desk. Have a Beautiful Day.

What if you're having a crappy day? What if you suddenly feel like you could implode?

Stupid. Stupid.

How did I screw up already?

Stupid girl.

I catch myself at my own words. I breathe out slowly. I pretend to put my hand at the side of my face as I look at my laptop, but what I'm really doing is taking my own pulse.

It's a bad habit I have when I'm stressed. Besides my flared nostrils that I apparently have at these moments, I'm also continuously checking if I'm still alive. Evan can read me like a book and makes fun of me when I do it.

Just relax, he would say.

Thinking of him makes me feel suddenly a little better.

Everything will be okay.

I suddenly remember Leigh's words of wisdom. Don't get on Nicole's bad side.

I sigh, thinking how silly I am. This isn't the end of the world, I remind myself. So what? I missed a meeting. Nicole will come to find out that it was a once in a career mistake. It won't happen again.

That's when I see him.

My man is standing by Leigh's desk in the flesh, waiting for her to get off the phone. I almost smile, wondering how it could be that Evan has appeared when I need him the most. It's almost out of my own desperation that I somehow conjured him up.

When Leigh puts the phone down, she beams at Evan. They have a quick exchange and Leigh points towards my office. She stands up but Evan waves her down and starts to walk towards me.

My savior.

Everything will be okay.

He stands outside the glass door and puts his face close to it, a hand over his head as if having trouble seeing me inside. I shake my head and laugh and he does the same before opening the door.

I stand up and want to kiss him, but the glass office makes me nervous to show public affection. "What are you doing here?"

"Not happy to see me?" he says with a smirk. "That makes sense, I'm only the love of your life, right?"

I grin. He comes closer, but before he can kiss me, I grab his hand at arm's length. "Not in the office," I whisper.

Evan looks outside at the rest of the staff, a few of whom are looking at him. I don't blame them. He's wearing a black button up shirt with dark pants and a beige blazer. His wavy dark hair is teased out perfectly. He smells absolutely amazing. It's a cologne I got him for Christmas.

"How can you work when everyone is watching you?" he asks.

Fair question, I think. "Did you just come to visit me?" I ask, changing the subject. I turn my head and notice Nicole watching us. I quickly turn my head back to Evan. He's right: everyone is watching, especially the boss. I better make this a quick interaction, even if all I want to do is be held by him.

"I wanted to surprise you," he says, putting out his hands. "Surprise." He laughs. "Well, maybe lunch. A quickie somewhere if you can pencil me in on your busy day."

I shake my head. I wish I could take him up on it.

"That all sounds amazing," I say. "And yes to that last part. I'll pencil you in when I'm done working and at home."

He smirks. "No fun. No fun at all. Please don't become one of those stuffy management types."

It's a comment he rubs me with from time to time, basically calling me boring.

"I love that you're here, I do," I say, "but today's not a good time." I turn my head slightly, but notice Nicole is not in her office. I look outside in the main area and spot her talking to Leigh.

Ugh. She must be laying into her now for missing the meeting too.

Evan tilts his head and grabs my shoulders. "Everything okay?"

I nod. "Just not a great day so far. You coming here makes me feel better though. I can't do lunch today. I just got in crap for taking a coffee break."

He shakes his head. "What kind of a place of work is this? I thought you office types live off of coffee?"

"We do, but not when it means missing an important meeting because of it." He looks at me with concern. "Long story, but it's okay."

I wait for his famous saying. "Just quit." Instead, he exchanges a look of worry of his own.

"I suppose now's not a good time to tell you that I spent our savings on materials for the reno?"

I almost want to scream. "What the heck did you buy?"

"Everything that we need. It all costs a lot. Tommy and I are working on the bathroom tiles next week. I'm finishing painting for the rest of this week."

I make a face. He told me last night he would have the painting done by tomorrow. "I thought you were going to be done sooner?"

"Well, Tommy and I got into a blow up; long story for me as well. I'll tell you about it when you get home. Just don't be late for any more meetings."

He laughs. “We sort of need the money.”

I almost feel like him being here made things worse. He looks at me and gives a thin smile. “Guess I’ll see you at home. I want to hear everything about what happened at work, and I’ll tell you about Tommy.”

He waits for me to kiss him or embrace him. I look outside and at the few faces catching glimpses of us and don't.

“See you soon." I grab his hand tightly. I let go and he turns to leave. “Wait,” I say to him. He turns to me with another look of concern. “Can you just say one thing to me before you leave?”

“Okay.” He laughs. “What?”

“Just tell me everything will be okay.”

He shakes his head. “Are you making a mountain out of nothing, Alice? Okay, this little issue you have at work, no matter how big you may think it is, is nothing.” He grabs my hands and stares deep into my eyes. “Everything will be okay.” He kisses my hand before leaving.

I watch as my handsome angel glides past the office staff. Some of the women turn their heads as he passes.

To my surprise, so does Nicole.

Even more surprising, her mouth is opening, and Evan has stopped in his tracks. He looks at her and back towards my office.

Suddenly his mouth opens too and the two are talking. What could they even be talking about?

My carefree husband looks back at my office, at me, and I see something I haven't seen in him in forever.

Fear. At least that's what it looks like. His tanned skin almost looks pale.

He nods at Nicole and walks down the hall. It's Nicole now who's staring into my office, directly at me, with a wide grin on her face.

CHAPTER 9

What was that about?

It's a question I continue to ask myself throughout the day. The face Evan had when he exchanged words with Nicole haunts me.

She was likely just introducing herself to him. But that wouldn't explain the weird expression he had before leaving.

Nicole hasn't come to my office for most of the day and it's nearly the end of work. I've been thinking of ways to go to her and nonchalantly gauge what happened. Any idea I can think of comes off corny.

I almost just want to go into her office and straight up ask, "Hey, what's with you and my husband?"

If it was a big deal, though, Evan would tell me. He would have texted me or called.

Although that's becoming a bit of a concern as well. I've called him on break once and texted him throughout the day when I have to use the bathroom. I have to be careful in this office. Everyone can see what I'm doing and Nicole knows

I don't have a corporate phone yet. Anything I do on my cell phone would obviously be personal.

I can only imagine how high my pulse rate would be if I used my phone and saw Nicole in her office staring at me.

Suddenly I wish I didn't have the spacious vice president office next to hers. The smallest one, well away from Nicole, would do just fine.

I catch my breath again and continue with my work until my door opens and Nicole enters. She's smiling at me.

"Are you busy?" she asks, and I try to find the right answer. If I say no does that mean I'm being paid big bucks to do nothing? I try not to overthink it and greet her back.

"Hey," I say with a smile. "Please, come in."

Nicole does and her expression fades. She puts the file she's carrying on my desk. "I had Leigh type up the minutes from today's meeting. There's some extra work that we have to get done tonight. It's going to be a long one."

What does that mean?

"Well," she says, sighing, "I guess you should get used to long nights. No rest at the top of the mountain. All the instructions on what I need you to do are in the meeting minutes. It won't be just you staying late but a few others, including myself. If you have any questions, just ask, okay?"

She waits for my response, but I'm still trying to wrap my head around that this workday won't be ending when I thought it would.

"Of course," I say with my own smile. "Whatever you need."

"Perfect," she says and turns.

"Any idea how long we may be in the office for?" I ask. "I'd just like to give a heads up to my husband."

She turns to me, beaming wider. "Well, as long as it takes for the work to get done. So since you're new here, I'm not sure how long that will take." Her smile wanes. "You're not one of those people who complain about putting work in?"

"Me? No, never. You can depend on me to do what's needed for this company anytime." I grab my phone. "I'll just text my husband to make sure he doesn't wait for me. Guess it's a pizza night for him."

"Don't make me jealous," Nicole says. "I need to leave the office for a little but will be back soon. Make sure to speak to the night security guard before you leave. They can walk you to your car if you're worried about that sort of thing... and by the way, Evan's a good man." She quickly turns and storms out of my office before I can ask her more.

CHAPTER 10

Nicole

Despite my entire world crumbling around me, seeing Evan's expression when he encountered me in the hallway made my day much better.

I may be going to jail any day now, but the look of shock on his handsome face will be a memory I keep with me in my cell for as long as I have left in the free world.

Making my day slightly better was Alice's reaction as well. The total look of confusion the woman had makes me nearly laugh out loud, until… I literally laugh loudly.

I'm in my car alone, though. I could barely contain myself as I walked into the foyer past security, nearly giggling to myself as I entered my car.

I laugh again, striking my steering wheel.

It's just too good.

I thought I was looney for hiring Alice, knowing who her husband was. I thought it was crazy for hiring a private investigator to tell me everything they could about Evan and Alice's life.

They seemed so happy in the brief the PI provided me.

That's nice for them.

It only pisses me off, though.

Now that I'm near the end of my professional life, I can't stop thinking about how some of the worst decisions I made were all because of Evan Walker. Now, Alice will find out the worst decision she made was to work for me.

When I saw Evan walk past me while chatting with Leigh, I immediately called out to him.

"Evan? Is that you?" I asked coyly. Of course it was. He smiled and turned to me. That smile immediately vanished as mine grew.

I followed it up by saying, "No, wait, you're not Alice's husband?"

"Hey, Nicole," he managed. "You work here?"

"I'm the president of Lovely Beauty Supplies."

That's when he made the face that will be ingrained in my memory. The look of shock was priceless.

"That's great," he finally said.

"Hey, how's your brother Tommy doing? And your family? I hope you give them all my best."

"I will," he said curtly. "I have to go." I watched him leave and push the elevator button numerous times frantically until the door opened.

Seeing Alice's confusion when I looked into

her office made it feel oh so satisfying.

What Evan knows, which Alice is yet to find out, is how terrible life will be for the Walkers. I'm back in his world. This time, there's no running. This time he will have to confront what he did.

Evan knows it could ruin his happy little marriage once his overachiever wife finds out about his past.

Alice Walker staying late for unpaid hours of work is the least of the problems to come.

home?

Perhaps he's badly injured and in a hospital bed somewhere. Wouldn't the hospital have called me by now? What if they don't have a way of identifying him to tell his wife what happened?

Sometimes I let my mind race when I'm worried and it always comes up with the most ridiculous ideas; it's always the worst-case scenario.

I'm a widow. My whole world is about to fall apart, and I don't know it. I can tell I'm anxious since my finger is already checking my pulse. If Evan was here, he would no doubt point out my nostrils flaring.

Of course, the worst-case scenario is never the reality. Instead, Evan is likely working on the house, busy. Maybe he lost track of time. He could have lost his cell phone.

All of these scenarios make so much more sense than he's dead or something terrible has happened. Is that something normal people think about, or is it just me that automatically thinks the worst without the slightest hint of danger?

A noise outside my office startles me. When I look out through the wall, I see nothing, though.

"Hello!" I call out. Nobody answers.

I wonder if it's the night cleaner. Maybe I can ask him if Steve, the day janitor, left my photo in the cleaning office.

Now this is a situation where I know the

most likely outcome is that the beautiful picture of Evan and I is in the trash underneath someone's spaghetti lunch somewhere.

I lower my head to my computer again, taking in a task sheet that I created to track the effectiveness of our most recent ad strategy. I noticed during our first meeting and from reviewing the notes from the previous executive of sales that they didn't have a proper metric for reviewing sales from individual marketing efforts we're trying. Hopefully I can present this to Nicole soon, maybe even at the next meeting.

I hope Nicole will love it. It could be useful. I only thought of it about thirty minutes ago when I finished my work and was tired of twiddling my thumbs at my desk.

I don't want to just leave, though. I've been waiting for Nicole to show up so that I can tell her all the work's done and make sure it's to her satisfaction.

I finally make my executive decision to leave. I can stick a note on the file folder I've been working on tonight and leave it on her desk. Hopefully the door is unlocked. I'll even make sure to write the time on the note. That way she will know I didn't just go quickly.

I put my time in tonight.

Or would that be a bad idea? I'll look pretentious for including a time. It's almost like a slap in the face. I was here at eight at night and you weren't, so I left.

How late does Nicole stay at the office anyway? If I'm using the sensible person test, I'm sure most people in my shoes would think something came up and Nicole has no intention of coming back tonight. She's likely already at home relaxing. Meanwhile I'm still here, working.

I stand up from my desk and sort the paperwork into the folder. I take a sticky note and write, 'All finished, Nicole. Please let me know if you need anything else,' and smack it on the top of the folder. I decide to leave out the time.

Thankfully, her office isn't locked. As if I'm in a place where I'm not supposed to be, I sneak into the room and place the folder gently on her desk.

I turn off the lights on the floor before I leave, looking around at the empty desks and offices before going to the elevator. Once on the main floor, I pass a night security guard who's at his desk. I startle him as he hears my footsteps coming down the hall. He quickly takes out his AirPods from his ear and greets me.

"Have a goodnight, miss," he says, nodding.

"Thanks so much. You too," I say with a smile.

"Would you like me to walk you to your vehicle?"

I look outside the building. The tinted windows make it seem darker outside than it is, but I know from being in my office that there's a bit of daylight left.

"I'll be okay," I say. "Thanks though." I leave the building and take a deep breath. The air is so much fresher after you're cooped up in an office for an entire day.

I look around the near-empty street. A man and a woman walk past me. For whatever reason, I say hi to them and they look at me as if I'm an alien.

Vancouver is a large city. I should be used to what city life is like. You don't just walk around smiling and greeting everybody like a psycho.

For a moment, I nearly forget where I'm parked. The lot is about two blocks from me. I stare down the darkening street. The tall buildings make it more dimly lit. I look above at dark clouds forming and realize I could get pummeled with rain any minute.

I feel uneasy again. I almost want to go back to the security guard to have him walk me to my car and realize I'm being silly. It's only two blocks away.

I look up at the buildings and their illuminated windows. In some I can see people moving. I might feel like I'm the only one on this street but I'm not the only person here.

I start walking down the block, taking quick glances at my surroundings. I hear a raised voice, and see the source as I pass an alley. One man is standing very close to another, his finger pointed into his chest.

Whatever they're talking about doesn't seem friendly, and I quicken my pace, hoping that they don't pay any attention to me.

I turn my head slightly back just to make sure they're not there. When I look forward again, I smile until I notice a silhouette of a person ahead of me. They are standing in the middle of the block, unmoving, looking in my direction. I lower my head, wondering if I should go back to the office. As I get a little closer, I notice they're standing beside a bush, nearly out of sight. I stop walking and stare at the person, wondering what I should do.

I know Toronto, while being a beautiful metropolis, can be dangerous as well, and a woman walking alone at night by herself isn't exactly a hard target. I'm overthinking this. This random individual isn't waiting for me.

I see the person near the bush put something in their mouth, and a red tip glows in the dark.

They're smoking, and for whatever reason, the cancer-causing substance gives me relief.

They just needed a cigarette. They aren't waiting for me. The person probably lives in the building they're leaning against. I try not to stare at the dark figure when a woman's voice makes me jump.

"Alice!" I turn and Nicole Barrett is gazing at me oddly. "Did you forget where the parking lot is or something?" She laughs.

"Nicole, hey," I say, taking a moment to look back where the silhouette person was. I'm surprised when I don't see them. Did they walk down an alley? I look back at Nicole. "No, I know where it is, thanks."

"Finished work already?" she asks with a funny tone. When I don't answer immediately, she grins. "I'm just joking. Did you finish the work I asked of you though?"

"Of course, and I put it on your desk," I say. The smoking person still isn't there.

"A little freaky at night," Nicole says, looking in the direction I am. "Next time just ask security to walk you. They are more than happy to."

"Thanks, Nicole. Maybe I will."

"Well, I have more time to put in tonight," she says. "I'm not sure I ever sleep, but then again, there's a reason why I'm who I am, and—" She looks around the surrounding buildings, many with windows illuminated by television sets. "—not them. I put in the work. I see that you are similar to me with that respect, Alice. I like that about you."

I grin. I can't hide how happy her comment makes me feel. The worries of missing the meeting today are almost immediately out of my mind. "Thanks, Nicole. I think we have a lot in common as well."

She smiles at that. "Evan is another similarity between us, which I was surprised to find out."

My mouth drops open a moment. "How do you know him?"

Her smile widens. "Oh, I know him well." She

laughs. Her giggle upsets me in the moment, but I shrug it off when I'm reminded that she's my boss. "I'll let him tell you, though. Seems like you two need to talk." Before I can say another word, she turns. "I'll see you bright and early tomorrow."

"Goodnight," I call out to her. I watch her as she calmly saunters down the darkened block. No concern at all. She isn't looking blocks ahead of her like I was, her head on a swivel. She isn't stopping when I see the pair of men walking the opposite direction towards her. She doesn't even seem to care that she's wearing expensive clothes, with her Gucci bag slung over her shoulder.

Not a care in the world.

It nearly makes me feel ashamed how cautious and anxious I am walking at night. A woman like Nicole likely never has to ask security to walk her to her car.

And somehow this woman knows my husband. How?

They could have been friends when they were younger.

The laugh she gave just now when I asked her makes me cringe. Were my husband and her intimate? A one-night stand? An old fling? All of these options sound terrible.

I turn to look at the parking lot and spot my car. Walking quickly towards it, I'm determined to find some answers.

CHAPTER 12

I park on my street and stare at my house. It's heavily raining outside now. Not a single light is on down my block, which I find strange. I expect that when I get inside, Tommy and Evan will still be working.

I remind myself that Evan mentioned something happened between him and Tommy. I'm sure he's upset about that, but I need to know what the connection is between my boss and my husband. I can't lay into him immediately about it.

I should start with a *so, how's your day? Did you get a lot done with the renos today without Tommy? Why did you and your brother fight?*

Then I can lay into *what the hell happened with you and Nicole?*

I imagine all sorts of possibilities. I still can't get Nicole's laugh she gave to me outside the parking lot. It was as if she knew it was juicy gossip.

So what if Evan and Nicole knew each other? Worse case, they dated. Why should I care? I wasn't a saint of a woman before dating Evan. It wasn't hard for me to figure out that Evan knew his way around a bedroom. He's drop dead gorgeous. A man who knew what to do with a woman.

So what if Nicole and my husband had… sex before we were married?

I could get over that. Nicole thought it was mostly funny anyway, at least from her laugh.

It must be super awkward for her too. How could she know Evan was my husband? He's from Ontario, and me, British Columbia. I'm from across the country, and Evan's last name, Walker, isn't exactly unique.

Nicole must have been just as surprised as me to find out Evan was my husband.

In some weird way, this could help us get along better.

I look at my dark house again, wondering if Evan is even home. It's nearly ten at night. Where else would he be? He hasn't called me back all day.

I lock my car and go up the steps. The house is still so new to me that I nearly knock on the door as if I'm a stranger here, but quickly remember to take out my keys. I open the front door and the room is pitch dark, except the dim light from a fire detector near the kitchen.

"Hey!" I call into the darkness. "Evan? You here?" Nobody answers.

I turn on the living room light, hoping to find Evan passed out on the couch or some sign of life in my house.

I instantly think of Tommy. Whatever

happened with his brother today, he must be trying to reconcile with him right now. He's likely at his brother's house. What else could he be doing?

I take out my phone and text his brother.

"Hey, Tommy. Is Evan with you?"

I take off my shoes and jacket, waiting for a reply. I stare at my phone every few moments hoping for Tommy to tell me where my husband is.

When my cell rings, I immediately pick it up. "Hey," I say into the receiver.

There's no answer. "Evan?" I say. "Tommy, is that you?" I turn my cell and see it's a private number calling. I put the phone back to my ear. "Hello?"

For a moment I hear the faint sound of breathing before it disconnects.

This isn't the first breath call I've received lately. If it was a prank call, wouldn't they have given up by now? If it was a scammer, wouldn't they want something from me? Say… something.

I realize I'm alone in my old rustic house, half torn down by my husband and his brother. I immediately turn on every light I can. I open the basement door and stare down into the dark. For whatever reason, maybe out of fear, I call out for Evan, but of course he isn't there. Why would he be in a dark basement alone?

My husband doesn't work. His brother isn't answering me. Where could he be?

I'm beginning to feel anxious again, just like

I was near the parking lot, only this time there's no security I can call. A streak of lightning flashes outside, followed soon after with a boom of thunder.

I put on the television and grab a bag of chips, trying to calm myself, when my cell buzzes. I look and it's Tommy. I drop the bag of chips to immediately check his message.

"He's not here. I haven't seen him since this morning. I'll tell him you're looking for him if I hear from him."

I lower my phone, my half-chewed chips still in my mouth. I look at the time. I've been watching television waiting for him to come home for over an hour. I have to wake up early tomorrow for work again.

I don't even care whatever happened with Nicole and Evan, I just need to know he's okay.

In a last-ditch effort, I call Evan's phone one more time. I pray for him to answer. That's when I feel a slight vibration under the pillow I'm leaning against on the couch. I look behind me and can feel a phone. It's Evan's.

I end my call now that I know my attempt to reach him is useless.

Evan left his phone at home and went out? That's not like him. He's usually joined at the hip to this thing.

I almost panic. I think of calling the police but wonder why I would jump to such an extreme.

What would I even say?

Help me, my husband left our house without his cell? Definitely not an overreaction.

I try to calm myself by watching more television, but the reality TV show isn't helping my mood. I turn it off and head up the stairs, turning on every single light that I can along the way.

I get to the bedroom and of course our bed is empty. I slip into the sheets, keeping the bedroom door slightly open with a light on my bedside table on to keep me calm.

I'm not sure how long it takes, but eventually I close my eyes and don't open them for some time.

When I do, the room is completely dark. I turn my head and see the light in the hallway is off. A sound beside me startles me, and I hear a laugh.

"It's me," Evan says, standing beside the bed. He slips his shirt off and jumps into bed with his jeans still on.

I hit him in the shoulder. "You scared the hell out of me. Where were you?"

Before he answers I can smell the beer on him. "Went to this local bar."

"Alone?"

"Yeah," he says, making a stretching sound. "I don't exactly know too many people out here."

"Why? Why did you drink alone? That's not like you."

He exhales and makes a spitting sound. "Because," he says curtly, "I can have a beer if I need to decompress, right?"

"Is it Tommy that's bothering you? The fight you had with him? What happened?"

He exhales again. "Not worth getting into. We're brothers, though. I'll call him tomorrow and we'll get over it. It's okay."

I touch his bare back and rub the hairs on his chest. I immediately feel better.

"How do you know Nicole?" I ask, not beating around the bush. It's late, I'm tired, and I need to know.

"Did she tell you anything?" he asks.

"She told me I should ask you," I say. I sit up in bed and rub the top of his shoulders. "So, tell me." I laugh.

"We were a *thing*... back in high school."

"High school?" I say. "Nicole lived in your town growing up?"

"Yeah. we dated a few years in high school, and a few years after too, but it didn't work out."

"What happened?"

He exhales again, and I take in a whiff of the strong odor of beer. "We are just different people." Understatement of the century.

"So you two were, what? High school sweethearts?"

He laughs. "I guess you could say that. Did your day at work get better?" I hate him for changing the subject.

"Well, it did. Nicole and I talked afterwards,

and I think things are good again."

Evan nods. "Is it going to be hard working at your new job now that you know Nicole and I were a thing back in the day?"

"We're adults," I say. "I mean, she's a bigshot president of a company now. She moved on from the great Evan Walker."

He lowers his head. "Will you leave me too?"

I'm taken back by his comment, wondering why he would even suggest something like that. "No, of course not. You're my husband."

He nods. "I'm beat. Goodnight." He kisses me quickly, and turns over.

That wasn't the kind of kiss I wanted from my husband, though. I've been waiting to see him all night. Since he surprised me in my office, I've been wanting to see him.

I want him. I rub his back and kiss his shoulder.

"I'm tired, Alice," he says. I put my hands at my side.

Again, not like my husband to turn me down. How much did he drink at the bar?

"Goodnight," I say to him. I roll over to the other side and face the wall. "It's okay that you went to a bar tonight, alone. Next time can you just text me or call me to let me know where you are? I was worried."

He doesn't reply immediately. I'm about to repeat myself when he finally answers. "Okay, boss."

CHAPTER 13

When I open my eyes, the bright sun through our bedroom window is nearly blinding. Usually, I close the blinds but in my franticness at being alone most of the night yesterday, I forgot.

I turn to look at the alarm clock on the nightstand beside me and nearly freak out when the lights on it are blinking. I look outside and realize it's way too bright to be six in the morning. When I grab my phone and look at the time, I nearly scream when I see that it's past seven.

The storm must have taken out the electricity last night, and my alarm. I usually put on my cell alarm too, but forgot last night. I could blame Evan's disappearance for that as well.

I jump out of bed and Evan wakes up calmly, stretching in the sheets. "What time is it?" he asks.

"I'm so late!" I freak out. I run to the washroom and get ready as quickly as possible.

Evan walks into the bathroom and opens the toilet lid, unleashing his full bladder of processed alcohol into it.

"Do you want me to drive you to work?" he

asks, yawning.

I don't answer him. For being such a manly man, Evan is kind of a slow driver. I'm used to city driving in Vancouver. I may be a very polite business professional, but when I'm on the road, especially going to work, I'm anything but nice. You have to be ruthless.

Today is not a day for my rule-following husband to get me to work; I'll be even more insanely late.

I break my own record for getting ready for work. For an executive manager at a cosmetic beauty company, I look like complete garbage today. Not exactly the image for someone in my role.

I'm certainly not having a "Beautiful Day" so far.

I kiss my husband as he's brushing his teeth, making a face when I make contact with his minty toothpaste.

He says something inaudible until he spits into the sink. "Have a good day!" he shouts as I run out the door.

I take pride in going to work early, or on time. I'm rarely ever late, unless sick or dying. With my mess up of missing the meeting yesterday and being late today, I'm not making a very good impression.

Now that I know that Nicole and Evan were high school sweethearts, I wonder how that will change the dynamic of our working relationship. Will she be even more critical of me or will our mutual connection with Evan help?

I think about it as I weave through traffic and pound on my horn, trying to navigate the intense streets of downtown Toronto. Luckily, I manage to get to the parking lot in record time, but I'm thirty minutes late.

I run as quickly as I can to my building and when I enter it, I wave at the security guard before frantically hitting the elevator button. At my old place of work, I would have run up the stairs, but that would be a little difficult now being on the thirtieth floor. When the elevator doors open, I step inside and catch my breath, fixing my hair before I realize I have not pressed which floor I need to go to.

As the elevator moves up, feeling slower than usual, I take in a deep breath, trying to calm my nerves. I take out my cell phone, and open the camera, looking at myself to fix any stray hairs from the quick bun I made when I rolled out of bed.

I hate not taking a shower in the morning. I feel dirty going to work without being clean. The times I haven't, I've worried that somehow people know I haven't showered, and I've felt like I stink even though my perfume would disguise what little odor I could possibly have.

When the elevator door opens on my floor, I calmly walk out of it, taking my time to greet a few coworkers as they pass me.

When I walk past Leigh, I wish her a good morning, and she does the same back to me. I look into Nicole's office and immediately feel overjoyed when she's not behind her desk.

I'm now forty-five minutes late, but Nicole isn't in her office to notice it. If I'm at all lucky, maybe she's running late herself.

I wonder how late she was working last night. She arrived as I was leaving. Maybe she's taken the morning off and will come later in the day.

My dreams are shattered when I see Nicole sitting at my desk. I swallow a little too hard while trying to maintain my composure.

What the hell am I going to say to her? Excuses seem weak. I tell myself I'm going to just apologize for my mistake. I won't get into details. She likely doesn't care what they are. She doesn't want excuses, at least I never did when the people who worked for me did something I didn't approve of.

I open the door, and Nicole's face lights up. She stands and greets me good morning.

"I'm sorry I'm late," I tell her. "It won't happen again."

She waves me off. "No problem, Alice. That's okay. I'm very curious though, how did your conversation go with Evan last night? Is that too much to ask?" She laughs. "It was just surprising for me to find out he's your husband, so I have to know."

I laugh, trying to not make it awkward. Nicole has a wide grin on her face. Part of her must think this whole situation is funny. She doesn't appear upset or trying to make me feel awkward.

"Yeah, we talked." I smile back. "He told me how you two were high school sweethearts a long time ago."

Her complexion changes, almost like she put a sour treat in her mouth. "Well, I suppose that's one way to describe your former fiancé." She laughs. "I would think he would just say that I was his fiancé though. Oh, Evan. Hasn't changed. God bless you for what you have to deal with." She laughs again, but I'm not smiling.

Evan didn't say a word about them being engaged. He made it seem like a wholesome high school situation. Nothing but young love. Now I find out the two were planning to marry.

"He didn't tell me that," I say, confused.

"Yeah," Nicole says. "I can tell from your expression. You should never play poker, darling; you would be bad at bluffing. That's Evan, though. A man of few words. I suppose we were not engaged for long, but still..." She lets her words dangle in front of me, not finishing her sentence.

"Is this going to be weird for us?" I ask, getting straight to the point.

"Evan and you?" she says innocently. "Of course not. That was literally a decade ago. I've moved on, and so has he. I'm happy for you two. I have to say, though, that my mouth nearly dropped when I spotted him in our lobby the other day." She laughs and I join in this time. "That was surprising to say the least."

"I bet." I laugh again. "It was for me too," I say. "Thanks."

"For what?"

"Not making this weird, because it is." I laugh again.

She nods. "It's not, though, really. I know what I want, and at that time, it wasn't Evan. I'm glad we seem to both have made the right decisions for ourselves." She gives me a thin smile and stares at me. "So, where is it? Did you leave it in the car?"

I'm not sure what she means, until it hits me. "Oh, no, your dry cleaning," I say, putting a hand to my head. "I can't believe I didn't grab it for you." I give a thin smile back to her, but this time it's not shared.

She looks at me sternly. "I assumed you were late because you were picking it up for me." She waits for me to answer, but I don't have anything but bad excuses. "Not only are you late," she says in a raised voice, "but you didn't even do what I asked of you." I lower my head and take a moment to glance outside. I spot a few people looking into my office. I can't blame them for watching the show.

Leigh is one of them. Even from all this way I can spot the look of worry on her face.

"I'm sorry, Nicole, I really am. I—"

"No," she says, cutting me off. "I need to depend on you. Even if it's small things, like doing me a favor, or, say, coming to work on time." She lowers her head, and when she looks at me again, she's beaming as if she was never upset to begin with. "It's okay, Alice. I just need you to be more on the ball here at LBS. I had high hopes for you when I hired you. Now..." She looks at her watch. "You have just enough time to leave the office and grab my clothes before our meeting at ten." Her smile widens. "So leave, now, and be fast." Her face sours again. "You can make up for the time you'll be missing after work. And don't be late for the meeting... please."

CHAPTER 14

Another late night in the office, but this time I'm getting out before the sun is setting at least.

Nicole had made me stay several hours past work. Not only did she have me "make up" for the hour I missed at work to pick up her dry cleaning, but I had to stay for a few more hours for no reason at all.

I'm starting to realize that my job may have a lot of unpaid time.

It was just me in the office again. It seems the only person that has to work late is me.

Thankfully, Nicole and I only had a few run-ins with each other after the initial exchange. I can understand why she's upset. I'm supposed to be there on time, and when I wasn't, she assumed it was because I was doing her a "favour" by running her errands.

It still irks me how she raised her voice at me. When I was in any leadership role, I never belittled anyone who worked for me. I made them feel like part of the team. I didn't put them down, make them feel small, or make them pick up my freaking dry cleaning.

Who the hell does that?

Part of me wants to hand in my resignation immediately.

I moved to an entirely new province, across the country, for this job, and it's not going the way I hoped. Nicole is something out of a horror movie. Smiling at me nicely one moment and jumping down my throat the next. Having me put in extra hours at work when no one else is.

To make things much worse, now I find out her and Evan were engaged to be married.

I tried to call Evan in the morning, while I was driving frantically to pick up Nicole's clothes from the dry cleaner, to demand he tell me everything that happened between my boss and him. Thankfully, he didn't pick up the phone, because if he had, I would have been just as intense as Nicole was to me in my office this morning.

Engaged!

How could he fail to tell me something important like that?

Was being engaged to a woman just not a big deal to Evan? Did he treat promises to be married like jobs and quit before he got to the altar? How many other women did Evan ask to marry?

It was only after I got back to the office that Evan called me back several times during the day, but I couldn't pick up. Not with Nicole in the office beside me. While taking a quick bathroom break,

I snuck in a text to him saying I would talk when I got home, and that I would be late again. He responded by giving me a thumbs up emoji.

I hate it when he does that. Can he not just reply with words? It seems lazy. Just like Evan.

Ugh.

Engaged.

Throughout the day, I replayed the intense exchange I had with Nicole. What made it worse was seeing how polite and fake Nicole seemed to be around others as the day progressed.

Besides the vice president who was fired the day I started work at LBS, I haven't seen Nicole treat anyone else as badly as me.

I thought of what Leigh told me at our coffee break. Don't get on her bad side. Was it already too late? Should I start packing up my office?

Before leaving for the night, several hours after I was supposed to be done, I reread the email from Nicole that was sent to the entire office. It was asking for email submissions for those interested in applying for the vice president position.

She had made it sound like I could be a good fit for it. She had a good feeling about me, she said.

That must have changed now.

I'm never one who needs to be reamed out at work. I'm never late.

But, apparently, now I am. Ever since moving to Ontario for this job, nothing is going my way. Or is it just me?

Stupid. Girl.

I can almost hear my father utter the words at me from beyond the grave.

I'm not good enough. I never was. Why did I think I would be a good fit for this position to begin with?

I was never meant to be a true leader, like Nicole.

Now, here I am in my late twenties, trying to be something I'm not. Trying to be what my father said I could never be. A success.

My father came from a time when women catered to men. A woman executive of a business was something he wouldn't understand. He would be blown away by the success of a woman like Nicole Barrett.

As I leave the office, I turn off the lights on the floor. I walk to my car in the parking lot, not even thinking of the potential dangers around every corner, but only of my failures during the day.

I don't have what it takes. I never did. Why did I ever think different?

I am a... stupid girl. I cringe at the thought.

I'm nearly in tears by the time I enter my car and turn the key. I take my time getting home, and when I do, I can already see Evan pacing around the house from outside.

At least my husband is home today and not at some bar alone.

I barely have enough energy to ask him

why he didn't tell me about Nicole and him being engaged. Why did he leave out that important detail of, oh yeah, we were supposed to be married?

Nicole was supposed to the original Mrs. Walker, not me.

I feel defeated. Someone could tell me the world was about to explode and it would fit today perfectly.

I open the door, and I can hear Evan's raised voice. "That's fine." He walks into the living room, his cell phone at his ear, and stares at me blankly. "I'll talk to you later." He ends the call on his cell phone and puts it in his jean pocket.

"Who was that?" I ask.

"Tommy," he says quickly.

"I take it you two didn't make up?"

He shakes his head. "Not really, no. He didn't come today."

I look at his clothes. They are clean. Not a speck of dirt. I can immediately tell he didn't do any work on the house today. What has my darling husband done all day while I dealt with his ex-fiancé at work? The thought enrages me and I find the energy suddenly to ask him.

"Why didn't you tell me you were engaged to Nicole?"

He looks at me blankly again, then around the room as if to find an answer. I repeat myself, in a slightly more agitated voice.

He raises his hands in surrender. "I— You're

right, I should have. It's just, I mean we were only engaged for two weeks, and things ended."

I kick off my heels without taking my gaze off my guilty husband. "Who gets engaged for two weeks? You need to tell me everything that happened between you two."

He sits on the couch and looks up at me with soft eyes. I hate it when he gives me this look. He has an ability to make me melt like butter no matter how upset I am with him.

I unfold my arms and sit beside him on the couch. "You never told me you were engaged to another woman before," I say, my head lowered. I look at him. "Why didn't you?"

He shakes his head. "I guess I didn't want you to think poorly of me. Like I said, it was only for two weeks. I didn't want you to think that I'm some psycho that would propose to you and leave you a few weeks later."

I exhale. "So why did you do that to her?"

He nods. "She left me, actually. And I'm glad she did. She was upset that I had no drive in life, she said." Suddenly I remind myself of the arguments I've had with Evan about the very same subject. There was a time when we dated that I was worried about what a future with Evan would look like. One of my friends, before I agreed to marry him, even called him a loser. Well, actually, a "handsome loser".

I can understand why Nicole brought it up

with him.

"So she decided to leave you because you weren't working?" I ask.

He nods. "She, as you can tell, is a driven woman. She had big plans, even back then." He laughs. "You know it's weird, but she kind of reminds me of you, now that we're talking about this. You, though, are not anything like Nicole."

For a moment, I feel hurt by his comment. Did he mean that I can't be as successful as her? I don't have what it takes to be like her. I think he noticed my face and quickly clarifies what he meant.

"What I mean is, she's overbearing. She was very controlling." He puts his hand up in frustration. "She could be so angry one minute and a saint the next. I never knew which woman she was going to be that day. I only asked her to marry me because she said I had to. She expected it of me after dating for four years. I mean, I was only twenty! How the hell was I supposed to be some driven business-minded person like her at that age? She talked about a house. Kids. I just wanted to drink and have fun."

I try to keep myself from thinking that not much has changed in the past decade. I remember what he said to me last night about me leaving him.

"I'm not anything like Nicole," I agree.

"She's... can I say this? I mean she is, she's a bitch... ugh."

I give him a look of disapproval.

"Okay," he says, "sorry, I shouldn't have said that. She's just too much. We had so many fights, I can't even count them. We were toxic for each other. After she broke it off with me and gave me back the ring, I was distraught for maybe a day, and then amazed at how little feelings I had after someone I had dated for several years broke up with me. I remember telling Tommy how little I seemed to care about not getting married to her. He thought I was crazy. He always thought Nicole walked on water. Joked about how good-looking she was. I could tell he was jealous. He probably wanted a woman like her. He never saw the side of her that I did."

I think of how two-faced Nicole was with me at work today. I tell Evan about my day. The late hours. How she reamed me out in front of the office and smiled in my face after like it was nothing.

Evan sighs. "She hasn't changed. She's still… I won't say it."

"A bitch," I add. I hate calling other women that, but in my anger at what happened today, I feel the same as him.

"Just quit," he says finally.

"The house," I say, looking around. "The mortgage. Bills. We have no savings left."

Evans' face drops. "Well, maybe don't quit right away. You could just get a resume ready. Start discretely applying. I'll slow down on the renos and work. We could have an applying for new jobs party tonight." He laughs and I join him.

He grins at me, and I nudge my head against his shoulder. "Maybe I should get my resume ready. I don't know if LBS will work. I'm not having a 'Beautiful Day.'" Evan looks at me funny. "It's this stupid motto the company has. This receptionist at work, Leigh, they make her say it every time she ends a call. 'Have a Beautiful Day.'" I shake my head.

"Now I feel even worse for this Leigh girl." Evan laughs.

I give a thin smile. An intrusive image of Nicole and Evan kissing hits me. The thought of them being together, being intimate, hits me.

"I need to ask you something," I say. "Was Nicole... was she the first woman you were with?" He nods. "What about her? Were you her first?"

"Yes," he says, without saying another word.

I lower my head and change the subject. "I could try and get a management job elsewhere. If you're working too, we could get through this. What would you do for work?"

He takes in a deep breath. "I'll figure something out. Don't worry." He tilts my head up to him and kisses me passionately. Soon, a few kisses turn to more flirty advances. I'm halfway taking off his jeans by the time I realize the curtains in the living room are still open.

"Evan!" I shout. "The window."

He continues to kiss my neck, and I nearly

forget about it.

"Let's give the new neighbors a show," he whispers in my ear.

"Not funny," I say, smacking the back of his briefs.

"Alright, alright." He stands up, his pants down to his shins, and waddles to the window, making a show out of doing it. When the room is darkened and it's just us, he looks back at me with a devilish grin. "Now, where were we?"

CHAPTER 15

Nicole

He. Hung. Up. On. Me.

Who the hell does Evan think he is?

He's still a piece of garbage even now. I could hear Alice in the background coming home. I don't care. He didn't have to talk to me that way.

No man talks to me with the tone he does.

I wanted him to meet me at the bar near his house again.

He refused.

Okay, fine, but don't talk to me that way. Don't treat me like I wasn't the woman you wanted to marry at one point in your life. I meant something to him.

I still mean something to him.

The life Alice has with him right now could have been mine. After what we spoke about yesterday at the bar, I thought we could figure something out. Obviously, I was wrong about that.

After he hung up on me, I took out my high school yearbook. It took me some time to find it.

In one of the many pictures taken

throughout that year, a large one of Evan and me is at the center of one of the pages. His arm is wrapped around my shoulder, and he's kissing the side of my cheek. I can even see his younger brother Tommy, standing behind us, watching.

The picture was taken at the first basketball home game we had that year. Both Tommy and Evan played on the team. Both looked good in their jerseys.

I smile thinking of those times with Evan. It was a fond memory. I sometimes think about how life would have been different if we got married. Now, only when my professional life is about to implode and I could go to jail, do I realize my faults.

I should have become Mrs. Walker. So what if I would have been broke living with a man like Evan? I would have been happy. All the wealth and pretty things I buy mean nothing to me at this moment. It's only when something is about to be taken away from you that you realize how unimportant it was to begin with.

Evan and I could have had something special.

And yet he hung up on me.

And yet he walked out on me at the bar last night.

He will find out very quickly how bad of a decision that was for him. Hopefully he will change his mind about what I want.

Evan has plenty of skeletons in his closet

that I bet Alice doesn't know about. Being engaged to me was only one. I wonder what Alice will think of her husband once she knows it all.

Does she know how violent he can be? The things he's done?

Evan better make the right decision next time, or else.

I pick up my cell phone and wait to hear their voice. I'm angered when it's not answered immediately, until I hear them.

"What are they doing now?" I ask.

"They're just inside the house."

I sigh. "Can you see inside? What are they doing?"

There's a long pause. "Kissing."

I exhale. I hate thinking about what they will do next, until the voice on the other side of the phone all but confirms it.

"They just closed the blinds."

CHAPTER 16

Alice

I lay in bed, unable to wipe the grin from my face.

Somehow, even after years of being with Evan, he has this amazing ability to completely satisfy my sexual cravings nearly every time.

He may not be a wealthy man, or even hard working, but when the bedroom door closes, he gets to work. Employee of the month. Gold star.

The man is good in bed.

I watch him as he gets out from the bedsheets and walks to the bathroom right outside our bedroom door.

"Ah!" he shouts.

I sit up in bed immediately. "You okay?"

He nods and lifts his foot, examining it. "Stepped on a nail."

I shake my head. A victim of his own home renovation project. Sometimes I wish he had just as much determination to finish all the work in this house as he does satisfying me.

"When is Tommy coming to help you

again?" I ask.

He drops his foot back to the floor and gives me an awkward stare. "I don't know."

"You two have a way of not getting over things," I say. It's true. I hate how explosive his side of the family can be. They all show so much affection to one another but at the drop of a hat, everything can change. I have to admit though, if anyone was keeping score, it would be easy to see Evan as the victor in terms of who started it.

"We'll get over it," Evan says. I hear him continue down the hall. "Ah, again!" he shouts.

"Another nail?"

"No, it's this wire I pulled out."

I can't help but laugh. I slip out of bed, walk over to the dresser and start putting on comfy clothes. I sigh when I realize Evan didn't fully close the drapes. At least he remembered that when we started our sexual adventure in the living room.

We ended everything in the bedroom.

I smile, thinking of how amazing my husband is in that way. For a moment, I think of Nicole, then make a face of annoyance at myself for doing so.

Why am I thinking of my boss?

She was his first love. First woman he had sex with. The reason I'm so happy right now is because they practiced everything together.

Did he master his craft in the bedroom with her first?

Ugh.

The idea upsets me.

I can't keep working there. Evan is right. It's going to be extremely difficult, but even with no savings left, barely any money coming in except my paycheque, I need to leave Lovely Beauty Supplies.

I can't work there with Nicole, especially now that I know about her and Evan.

Every time I'm intimate with my husband, am I going to think of her? If not, I'll see her the next day at work.

I think about the way Nicole yelled at me in the office today. She had to know that everyone could hear us. In our invisible-wall workplace, they could even see us. It was belittling. She may as well have bent me over and slapped my rear in front of everyone.

Quitting is against my nature. It's not natural to me like it is Evan. I don't quit, ever. I get better. If I'm not excelling in a job, which is never, it's something I'm doing wrong. I fix what I need to fix about me.

This time, I can easily point the finger at someone else. Nicole Barrett.

I'm quitting because of my boss. I never thought I'd think of such a thing.

I've never been spoken to so harshly, though, and over what? Her dry cleaning. Why the hell is it up to me to even get it for her? I can feel my blood pressure rising and my face flush red at the thought.

Another intrusive thought strikes me. I have Evan. She doesn't.

Even if my husband learned his bedroom ways because of Nicole, she doesn't have him. He's my husband. I'm the lucky one here. I have a good man who can satisfy me and is usually willing to do so anytime I want.

It seems like a childish thought, but it makes me smirk knowing that Nicole can't have something I do.

I may be jealous of her in every single other way. She's president of a company. She's huge in the business world and revered by many for her entrepreneurial skills. The woman was on the cover of *Forbes Magazine*. She's business-savvy and knows what she's doing.

Nicole Barrett is essentially everything I want to be, but she doesn't have Evan. That much I have over her. No matter how much more abuse I have to take from her before I quit, I will smile at that thought.

I won't leave right away. I'll start secretly sending out resumes for other executive jobs. The problem with that, though, is there's a small group of people who run companies, and it feels like they all know each other.

They play golf together. They know each other's business. They talk. If you're not part of the club, you have no clue what they're saying about you.

I have to be careful about who I apply to. The last thing I want is for Nicole to find out. The last thing I want is to go back to work for a small company like what I had before.

Even though I've only been an executive member for a few days, I'm completely hooked on the job itself.

I have to find a way to continue to rise without burning bridges. That means Nicole as well. It's going to be difficult, but there will be a way to do it. I just have to look for my opening.

I stand by the large window and look out into the dark street. Thankfully my area is nothing like downtown Toronto. It's less scary in the dark. I see all the houses down the block, some with toys in the front yard, and feel more comforted.

I think of Nicole again and how she wasn't frightened like I was walking down the block near work at night. She couldn't have cared less that she was wearing her expensive clothes and purse. She could easily have been a target for criminals, but you wouldn't know it by looking at her.

It's because she's the predator. She's the shark.

I stare outside the window again, and for a moment see a large shadow standing near my front yard. A person. I look at the clock by my bedside. It's nearly midnight. I feel my heart beating faster, nearly exploding out of my chest when I look back out the window again.

I breathe out deeply, telling myself I'm overreacting. It's just a bush. I look at some of the other bushes in the yard. They could easily be mistaken for a human, especially at night. Our eyes can play tricks with us.

I look at the bushes, the wind breezing through their branches, causing them to move, except one. Suddenly it moves quickly. I see a hand in the dark as it hurries down the block.

I cover my mouth not to scream.

A hand grabs my shoulder and squeezes. Now I scream until Evan calms me.

"Whoa." He laughs. "I know I'm not good at massaging, but that's not necessary."

"Someone's outside." I point outside. "They were in our yard, looking into the house. When I noticed them, they went down the block."

"So they're gone?" he asks, confused.

"Why were they there?"

He shrugs. "Maybe a curious neighbor. Could be a guy walking his dog. Tomorrow morning I'll find some fresh poop on the lawn."

"Can you go check?"

"For what?" he asks, confused. "You said you saw them leave."

"Evan," I say, pleading with him. Could he not just do what I want him to without the resistance? This isn't me screaming at him to kill a spider. A freaking person was outside our house, in our yard.

“You always jump to the craziest conclusions, Alice.” He laughs.

“It scared me.”

He laughs again. "Well, you’re easily scared too.”

I turn to him with my dark eyes. “Please can you just look?”

He sighs. “Okay, okay.” He stands behind me, looking outside the window.

“No, can you go outside and check?” I roll my eyes.

He sighs louder this time. “Okay, okay.” He slaps my rear. “If I'm not back in ten, call the cavalry.”

CHAPTER 17

A week has gone by, and thankfully, nothing eventful has happened at work.

It's almost as if Nicole is an entirely new boss. Not the same person who belittled me in front of all the staff. No more requests for me to do her errands either. At meetings and at work, I've been treated well, not only by Nicole but the rest of the staff. No working late at night on my own.

Things have been great.

Even though it's something I don't tend to do, I'm even developing more and more of a friendship with Leigh. We've gone out for a few coffee dates. One even after work. We've exchanged numbers as well. She's a little younger than me, and is Nicole's executive assistant, but I have to say I really enjoy spending time with her.

I'm beginning to feel foolish for even thinking of leaving LBS. Perhaps my first week on the job was a fluke. Nicole could have been under a lot of stress, and for whatever reason, I got targeted.

Now, you wouldn't think anything was wrong at all.

The other day, Nicole entered my office just to let me know she thought I handled a project really well. I'm back to getting praise for my work.

It's almost as if things have turned a complete 180. Even though my resume is prepared, and I've been searching for positions that I believe Nicole wouldn't find out about if I applied for, I haven't actually sent a single one.

The aura at work has completely changed. I truly am having a beautiful day.

Nicole hasn't said a word about Evan as well. I thought it was going to be excruciatingly weird being at work around her, but it hasn't been. She never brings him up, and I don't either.

As I sit at my desk, completing my work, I can't help but think how silly I was for wanting to leave.

Evan told me that I tend to jump to the worst case scenario all the time. In my head, Nicole was a monster.

I'm beginning to think Evan actually has a point.

Things are getting better, not only for me, but for Evan as well. Tommy and him made up. His brother's been helping him with the renos on the house again. It's nice coming home and seeing the brothers share a beer.

We had a funny moment when Evan pointed out that Tommy's relationship status on Facebook changed from single to "it's complicated". He still refuses to tell us more about his mystery girl.

It's good to see him and Evan back to being brothers. I just hope that their camaraderie holds this time, at least until my house doesn't look like a construction site.

Leigh stands outside my office door and waves at me. I grin back.

"Good morning," she says.

"Hey!" I say back. I shake my head. "So, you have to tell me about how your date went last night. You never texted me back. I have to know. You told me the man had a neck beard? I had to look that up to see what it was."

Leigh's face sours. "Ugh. Don't even remind me. That's what I get for trying internet dating. The profile picture looked nothing like the man that met me at the restaurant. I made it through dinner with him without shaving his face, but, yeah, he wanted to drive me home. I said I drove and took an Uber." She laughs. "Yeah, now I'm worried about the date I have this Saturday from the same website."

I shake my head. "What does a woman like you need dating sites for?"

She laughs. "Not all of us are so lucky to be married to a hunka hunk like you."

I shake my head at the remark. "If you knew Evan like I did, he would be less hunky and more annoying."

Leigh gives a thin smile. "All men are."

"Our two-year anniversary is tomorrow."

"Oooh, how nice," she says playfully. "What are you two lovebirds doing?"

"A nice restaurant, and we'll see where the night takes us."

"Hopefully back to the bedroom," Leigh says with a laugh.

I grin. "I tell you way too much about my life, don't I?"

Leigh smiles back. "Well, it's a fair deal. You get to hear about my mess of a dating life." She looks outside the office into Nicole's and back at me. "Listen, Nicole asked me to arrange a meeting time for you and her today."

"What for?" I ask.

Leigh shrugs. "She didn't give me a reason. Should I ask her?"

"No, no. That's okay. Anytime works."

"The earliest she has is one."

I nod. "Perfect. Thanks, Leigh."

She waves her fingers at me. "Bye, girlie," she says. "Coffee break today?"

"Of course," I say with a grin. "My new addiction is the coffee place you brought me to, and it's all your fault. Today, I'm buying."

Leigh leaves my office, and I watch her walk back to her reception area. When I turn my head, I see Nicole staring into my office. She smiles at me before looking back at her computer.

The look she gave puts me off for some

reason as I slowly turn my gaze back to my screen.

What does Nicole want to see me for today?

I instantly think of the older woman with red hair, the former vice president. The woman who was terminated the day I started work at LBS.

Was I being fired? Why? For what?

For the issues I had last week? Did Nicole think I wasn't working out anymore for her company and wanted me gone? What would that mean if I was actually fired? It's something that's never happened before.

What would it mean to look for work while being unemployed? I'd be blacklisted from any new executive position, ever.

I calm myself, trying to think of what Evan told me. I'm doing it again. Jumping to conclusions and the worst outcomes.

Nicole has started chatting with other staff about the vice president vacancy. It could easily be about that.

I haven't applied for it, though. After last week, I assumed I didn't have a chance. Last week I didn't want to stay at LBS, so why would I apply for its second-top position?

I do my best to calm my nerves until our meeting, but it's excruciatingly hard. I don't go out for coffee with Leigh. I don't want to let her see me as the nervous wreck that I am. My nostrils flaring like a dragon or checking my pulse like a maniac.

I think of calling Evan, just to hear his voice.

Instead I focus, the best I can, on my work, and thankfully our meeting time comes, feeling like it took nearly a decade.

Just as Leigh had, I stand outside Nicole's glass door, looking in at her with a wide smile. I knock on the door, but Nicole doesn't look up at me.

"Come," she says.

The smile on my face vanishes. *Come?* Who says that to someone? What am I, a dog?

I do as she commands, and open her office door and step inside cautiously. "Hey Nicole," I say, feigning another smile. "How's your day?"

Now she looks up at me and gives me her own fake smile. "Such a busy one. I'm glad we're able to meet, though. I wanted to have a chat with you. So, you've been here for a little over a week. Big move for you too, coming from Vancouver. How are you liking it here?"

I try to avoid my frustration over last week and just focus on how I've felt since. "It's been great. You have a very welcoming staff here. Made me feel at home." That's true. Now if only Nicole wasn't nuts, my job would be absolutely perfect.

"That's great." Nicole shuffles on her seat, flattening her black skirt. "And Evan? How's he dealing with the move out here? He must be happy being reunited with Tommy. Those two were peas in a pod back in the day." Nicole laughs, and I feel like shrinking in my seat. Hearing my husband's name come from her lips makes me sick.

"Well, he's very busy renovating the house right now." I can hear my husband's voice in my head. Tell her to back off. Don't talk about personal life at work. If it makes you feel uncomfortable, ask her not to bring me up. Be assertive. I take in a breath before finding the words. I've only practiced this moment in the mirror for the past week. "If it's okay with you, Nicole, I'd like to not talk at work about my hus—"

"Why haven't you applied for the VP position?" she asks curtly, cutting me off. Her question throws me off.

"The position?" I ask, confused by why she's asking.

"Yes, I think you would be great for it, really." She smiles at me again. "You certainly have what it takes. Sure, you had a few screw-ups your first week, but your work speaks for itself. You put in the hours like no one else here does. I look for people that go the extra mile, and that's you. You've shown me that."

"I wasn't sure where I stood here at LBS, to be honest," I say. "I thought you weren't happy with how I was performing."

"Very much the opposite, Alice. I'm very happy with your progress. You're outperforming some of my veteran executives. Some of those people have that attitude that it's their turn, though. They have taken their time here for granted. I know this isn't the last place where you want to be, here at LBS. What are your true aspirations?"

I lower my head, and fix my skirt now. "Well, to be honest, you." Nicole beams wider. "I'm truly inspired by what you have accomplished, and for a woman so young." Nicole waves me off and laughs. "No, really. I'm always willing to put in the work, and go above what is needed to get to where you are. I would do whatever it takes. I want you to know that, Nicole."

"That's good to hear, because if you were to be a VP, especially at your *actual* young age—" This time I smile authentically back. "—a door to a president job could be yours within a few years. This job will open not just a few doors, but all of them."

The thought of it hits me.

"Now," Nicole says, sitting straight in her chair, putting a pen to her red lips, "I want to schedule a dinner date. A meeting, I mean. I'll call Evan to arrange it."

"Evan?"

"Right," she says, beaming. "I have his number here." She sorts through a pile of paperwork on her desk and takes out an employee information form I filled out on my first day. "He's your emergency contact, I see. I'll just speak to him about it."

"You want to schedule a meeting with my husband and I for dinner?"

"Just him."

I try to catch my breath. She brings me in here to talk about promotions and now she wants me to sit here while she talks about going on a date with my husband? She even called it a "dinner date".

"Why?" I say in a stern voice. I try to calm myself. Having this much anger directed at my superior is never something I've experienced.

"Well, to catch up. You tell me all about him. He sounds like he's doing well. I want him to tell me, though. Catch up."

"You want to go on a date with my husband?"

She points the pen at me. My instinct is to grab it from her and throw it at her face, but instead I sit there and listen. "I didn't say date, did I? Attention to detail, Alice. That's an important part of being VP. I want to catch up, I said. We were close. He was an important part of my life. It will be friendly, of course."

"But you want to be alone with him?"

"How can two people truly catch up if you're in the room?" She laughs. "Let's say tomorrow night after work. I don't want to schedule a weekend dinner. That sounds too much like a date to me." She laughs. "I certainly don't want to give you the wrong impression here."

Our anniversary dinner is tomorrow. I wanted to celebrate our marriage on the day we actually got married. There's no way this lunatic will see my husband on that day.

"Wednesday won't work," I say. I stand up from the desk, unable to hide my disgust for this woman. "None of this will work. He's my husband!"

"Calm your voice, please," Nicole says, making a gesture with her hands. "Please, act professional. This is our place of work after all, VP."

The way she throws the title in my face makes me sick. Does she think I'll pimp out my husband for a promotion?

"This is too far, Nicole. I can't work here any —"

"I would think long and hard about that," she says, standing up and meeting my gaze. "I'm talking about promotions with you today. A leading beauty supply company and you could be VP of it. Think hard about what that could do." When I don't respond immediately with disdain, she smiles. It quickly vanishes. "But imagine what could happen if you don't do what I ask. I know a lot of people, not just in Toronto. A VP needs to make decisions quickly sometimes. Show me you have what it takes. Or don't. Make your decision. Take a day to think it over, and then I want my answer."

CHAPTER 18

I haven't told Evan about today. I know what he'll say.

Quit.

I should. I know it. If I do, I'll be quitting everything I ever wanted.

Nicole didn't just threaten me about quitting, she basically told me she will ruin my career if I do.

None of this is legal. A boss using her power over an underling to get what they want. And what does she want?

That's plain as well. My husband.

My boss is completely unhinged. Thank goodness she dumped Evan when they were younger or else his life would be worse than I feel at this moment. As an employee, I get to check out from work. Imagine being married to her. Having to be around such a terrible person every day.

That would truly be hell.

How did Evan ever get engaged to someone like her?

I lay in bed, thinking of my meeting in

her office. I haven't been able to stop myself from replaying it over and over.

It was so crass. No beating around the bush. Give me your husband, or else.

A knock on the door startles me. Evan comes in holding a bowl and a cup of water.

"I made you soup," he says. "We only had tomato soup cans in the pantry though." He makes a sour face.

I smile at him as he places my dinner on the nightstand. I look at the soup and I'm amazed that he garnished it with a bunch of parmesan, the way I like it. I look up at him and feel sick inside, knowing what Nicole wants.

Evan sits on the bed beside my legs, rubbing my side. "Hey, you never told me how work was today?"

I take the cup of water and have a sip. Work and Nicole is the last thing I wanted to discuss.

"Okay," I say. I want to tell him. I know Evan, of course will be on my side, but he could make it worse. He's outspoken and aggressive. If I were to tell him, he would storm into LBS right into Nicole's office and give her hell. Or would he? I remember the face he had when he first spotted Nicole at my work. It was as if he had seen a ghost. I'm starting to be as petrified of Nicole as he is.

"You think it's just a bug?" he asks. "Whatever you have?" He shook his head. "Ugh, please don't give it to me. Maybe we should cancel our reservation tomorrow. The last thing I want is for my wife to be sick on our anniversary."

I look at him for a moment. I can feel my blood boiling over. That would be exactly what Nicole would have wanted. I'm celebrating my anniversary with my husband.

"No, I'll be okay," I say. "I'm already feeling better. I just needed rest, I think."

"Work stressing you out?"

More like work is the only thing stressing me out.

"Something like that," I say.

Evan puts his hand across my forehead. "Well, you feel okay." He makes a face again. "Maybe I should sleep on the couch. I don't want this, whatever you have."

I turn away from him. "Do whatever you want."

He pauses. "Hey, are you mad at me? I just don't want to get sick. That's all."

Part of me is mad, and I don't know why. I'm mad that my boss is someone he was engaged with. I'm mad that his ex is driving me crazy. I'm mad at myself for not immediately quitting.

Is my dream of being a woman in charge someday worth this?

I won't let Nicole Barrett take that away from me.

"I'm just feeling yucky," I say. "Sleep on the couch. It's okay. I don't want you to get this."

More like I don't want him to feel Nicole's wrath. I have my resumes ready. Time to start using them. Tomorrow I will start applying.

"Goodnight," he says, standing up. He bends near me and kisses my forehead. "Call me if you need anything. I'm just working in the bedroom down the hall for a few more hours."

"Thanks," I say, not turning over. I can't look at him. If I do, he'll know I'm truly a mess. If I stare into his beautiful eyes, I'll pour my soul out to him.

I lay in bed for some time, thinking more about Nicole and what I should do tomorrow.

An image of me storming up to her and slapping her in the face as hard as I can makes me feel better, but of course it's not realistic.

Quitting is a much better option, and one that won't land me in handcuffs.

My cell phone buzzes under the bedsheets, and I answer. "Hello?"

Again, I'm met with silence. I know someone is there because I can hear them breathing.

"Who is this?" I ask. "Why do you keep calling?" An image of Nicole holding my personal emergency information hits me. "Nicole? Is that you?"

I hear their breathing getting louder. I put my phone away from my ear and see the number is private. I put the phone back to my ear and the breathing on the other end is so loud, I pull my ear away from my phone. I hang up and drop it on the mattress.

I get out of bed and look outside at the dark skies and think of the person who was on my lawn last week. I stare at the bushes where I saw them. This time, all the bushes are moving with the wind in a normal way.

My phone buzzes again on my bed. The screen brightens, illuminating the dark room, showing a private number is calling me again.

This time I don't answer. I just watch as it continues to buzz until it stops, and the room goes completely dark again. I stare at my cell phone, waiting for it to light up again from the caller.

I catch my breath when it doesn't happen immediately. I stare outside the window as well, and while guarded about what could be outside, see nothing.

Then I hear the phone ring again, only this time it's not mine. It's faint but coming from outside the bedroom. It stops soon after, and I open the bedroom door slightly, hearing the near-whispered sounds of my husband.

"No, I won't," he says with intensity. "That's fine. I'm ending the call. I don't care what you do." I take a few steps outside the bedroom, and the old floorboards creak, alarming my husband. "Goodnight."

I walk down the hall and look into the guest bedroom where Evan is working. He is already off the phone now. He turns to me and smiles.

"Feeling better?" he asks.

I nod. "I guess. Who was that?"

"Tommy," he says. "He's coming tomorrow. I told him to come anytime."

I stared at him, knowing that wasn't what he said. "You said you don't care what they do."

Evan looks at me blankly. "Right. He said he wanted to come by around noon. I feel that's a bit late, but I mean, he's free help. Who am I to tell him what time to come by. Anytime is fine. I don't care."

I nod. "Someone's been calling my phone lately. They don't say anything but breathe into the phone."

Evan stands up from the floor, brushing off dirt from his jeans. "How many times?"

"It started a while ago. I don't know. Usually I just hang up. It's starting to scare me. And than there was that person outside our home last week."

"I checked outside. Whoever it was, they shuffled on. Like we said, it was probably a neighbor. Someone who lives nearby. They're probably curious who lives in this house now."

I nod again. "Right. I don't know. I'm just worried."

"About what?" he asks. I don't answer him. Evan grabs my hand softly and kisses it. "I'm here. You have nothing to worry about." He kisses my hand again.

"You know, I think I'm feeling better enough

for an actual kiss."

He smiles at me and gives me a soft kiss with no tongue, but of course I can't blame him for that.

I grin at him. "Can you sleep in the bed with me tonight?"

CHAPTER 19

Today I'm going to blackmail my boss,

That's never something I thought I would even think, much less actually do.

I sit in my office, building myself up for what at I'm about to do.

I could barely sleep last night, even with Evan in bed with me. His presence comforted me, even though it's technically because of him that I can't sleep. His crazy ex-fiancé is trying to manipulate my career to get to Evan. The idea made me sick to my stomach, even though I wasn't actually sick.

Late last night I searched for a recording app that I could quickly open and record with. At some point today, I'll walk into Nicole's office and tell her, to her face, no to her blackmail proposition for a date with my husband.

I'll record the conversation. I'll use that to sue her if I have to. I'll send it to every newspaper in Canada. A high-powered businesswoman like Nicole is sure to get enough buzz for them to want to print the story.

If she wants to play dirty, I'll make sure she can never get clean again.

I will tell her to her face about the recording afterwards. The hope is that she'll back off completely. I'll start applying for work quickly. Find a new executive job. Leave LBS as soon as possible.

I'll be able to keep my career and my husband without Nicole interfering with either.

My plan has its faults, like how I don't want to actually go through with it. It will put my husband and I in the public for everyone to judge. I'll be the subject of many people's dinner table conversations that day.

"Hey, did you hear about that woman who was blackmailed by her boss to sleep with her husband?"

I can picture it now, and the idea sickens me. Evan would hate it. I haven't exactly told him what I'm planning. I'm not going to tell him about this unless I have to.

He could make things worse. It's better I move on from LBS as quickly as I can.

It's nearly lunchtime, and Nicole hasn't asked for another meeting with me or called me into her office. I'm thankful for that. I need time to build up my confidence.

Truth is, I hate confronting people. This has to be the most extreme confrontation I will ever have.

If I make a mistake, it could mean my career.

What happens if I try to record the conversation and the app doesn't work? It should. I paid for it. I tested it at home before work and even in the parking lot before I entered the building. I know it works and how to use it.

I won’t tell Nicole about the recording until I confirm that I have our conversation saved and the audio is clear.

Without evidence, it would be my word against hers. Sure, an accusation could damage a woman like Nicole Barrett's reputation, but in the court of public opinion, there would be many who’d question if I was telling the truth. That’s only if I actually go public, which I pray I’ll never have to.

Every so often, I look into Nicole's office. She’s been there all day. I’ve seen her with her fake smile plastered on as she talks to staff that enter and when she’s on the phone. Seeing her face makes me sick. I can't believe what this woman is making me do.

It’s almost like she’s waiting for me to come to her with my answer. It’s as if she knows I have to say yes.

I take out my cell phone. I’ve been sneaking texts to Evan all day. My last text asked him how renos are going.

I felt my cell phone buzz a while ago but waited to look at it.

Evan: “Good. Getting a lot done today. Still waiting for Tommy to show. Not sure if he will. He says he's busy with this girl he's seeing."

I quickly respond. "When will we ever meet her?"

He responds immediately. "Pretty sure she doesn't exist." He followed the text with a laughing emoji.

I put my cell phone on top of my desk and rub my eyes.

I need to get this over with. No more hiding from what I have to do. Nicole isn't going to let up. She'll be relentless. I can see what Evan meant about her. She will do whatever it takes to get her way.

A knock on my office door breaks my thoughts, and I stop breathing when I see it's Nicole, a fresh fake smile plastered on her face, looking directly at me. Before I can grab my phone and open the app, she opens the door.

"Good day, Alice," she says. She steps closer to me. "And how are you today? I was hoping you would come by to see me."

I stare at my phone, wanting to grab it quickly. I already have the app open. I just have to hit the record button. The screen will go back to black as it does. It won't be noticeable.

"I'm okay, Nicole, how about you?"

"Well, just like our slogan, I truly am having a Beautiful Day." She laughs.

My phone buzzes on my desk and I quickly grab it. I can see it's Evan. "Sorry," I say as I open my phone and click the record button. I pretend like I'm reading a message. The app shows me a red number that's counting upwards, confirming that it's on, before the screen turns black.

"Sorry," I said again. "We're having a home reno emergency. Evan thinks he's a plumber and now we have some minor flooding."

"That's terrible," she says as she looks at my phone. "Knowing Evan, he'll believe that he can fix it." She laughs at her own joke. "So, I wanted to come by and ask. Have you had any more thoughts about applying for the vice president position, Alice?"

I smile. "Well, Nicole," I make sure to say her name clearly for the recording, "I thought about what you're doing and—"

"It's okay," she says. "I understand. I know it's a lot. You just moved to Toronto and now I'm asking you to apply for the number two job here. I just think you would be a great fit. If you ever rethink about it let me know. I'm just—" She points at her office. "—right there."

This isn't going the way I planned. Nicole was supposed to be spilling her guts to me. Getting upset. Repeating what she said yesterday. My phone is getting nothing but a friendly boss consulting me about my career.

I stand up from my desk. "What you said about my husband, Evan, is—"

She cuts me off again. "Alice," she says

loudly, “I know it’s awkward for both of us that you’re married to a man who was engaged to me. I told you, it’s fine. I’m okay with it. Him and I have both moved on. I’m glad he’s found such a lovely person to be his partner for life. It’s been years. You don't have to worry about it. Now, I have to get going. I have that big meeting with Warner coming up. They’re coming by tomorrow for a tour as well. That marketing material we talked about, did you finish it?”

I stumble again, trying to figure out a way to turn around this conversation back to her blackmailing me, but fail miserably.

“Well…” I sit stumbling on my words.

“Can you stay late tonight to get it done?” she asks, her fake smile growing even wider.

Tonight is my anniversary dinner. She doesn't know that, of course, but I won’t let her ruin my night.

“No,” I say in a lower voice. “I can't tonight.”

Nicole’s smile fades quickly, and she stares at me a moment before her wicked smirk returns to her face. “Not a problem. Thanks for the talk.” She turns and quickly leaves my office.

I lower my head and stare at my phone, which has secretly recorded one of the most pleasant exchanges I've ever had with a president of a company.

CHAPTER 20

Nicole has been gone for the remainder of the workday. It's nearly time to leave, and I haven't seen her since our conversation in my office.

The recording app worked perfectly, catching Nicole's voice easily, being on top of my desk. The problem is that it caught nothing of worth.

I remind myself that there will be other opportunities. A few times throughout the day, I secretly swear under my breath at myself for my bare-faced lie about Evan busting a water pipe. Did I make it too obvious that I was recording the conversation? I'm not exactly very good at attempting to blackmail my boss. I wonder why it comes so naturally to Nicole.

That sick feeling in my stomach has returned.

What the hell do I do now?

Evan needs to know what's happening. He needs to know what his crazy ex-fiancé is putting me through.

Tonight, at our anniversary dinner, I'll tell

him everything. No more keeping secrets. We're married and we need to be a team about this.

I hate the idea that on a day celebrating our marriage, we have to spend it talking about his ex-fiancé. Instead of having a happy day reminiscing about our love story, we'll focus on how a former lover is ruining everything in my life.

The buildup to the confrontation with Nicole was enough to make me physically ill. Thinking about having another difficult conversation with Evan today makes me nauseous.

Thankfully, the restaurant isn't too far away from the office. We made reservations for soon after work was done. I'll see Evan soon. I'll get everything off my chest about what's happening and the mess that I am in because of it. I know he'll raise hell. I imagine if it was him having to confront Nicole today, he wouldn't bother with a recording device. He would scream and shout at her, while everyone listened. No need for a listening device because everyone would witness what's happening.

I sigh, thinking how I should have handled the conversation with Nicole better.

A knock on my office door breaks my sorrows. I half-expect Nicole to be there again, tormenting me further, but instead it's Leigh. She waves at me before entering.

"Hey, what gives?" she asks. "No coffee this morning. And barely a hello." She grins at me. Hers is so much more authentic than our boss's. When she sees my face, her happiness fades. “Everything okay?”

“Well, not really, I guess,” I say. I think about telling her about Nicole. How would she react if I did? Would she be on my side? Nicole is her boss too.

No, I won't involve anyone else in this mess. Leigh has been nothing but good. I won’t drag her down with me.

“It’s my anniversary today with Evan,” I say.

“Oh,” she says, confused. “Shouldn’t you be happy then?”

I give a thin smile. “Yeah, I am. It’s just been a day, you know?”

Leigh nods in agreement. “Nicole has been on my ass all day. I think she’s worried about that meeting today. She’s been at the Warner Group across town all day.”

“They’re coming tomorrow to the office too, I hear,” I say.

Leigh sighs. “Yeah, and I get to work late tonight. Nicole needed me to do some extra work.”

I wonder if turning down the after-hours work Nicole wanted me to do has anything to do with Leigh staying late.

“Sorry,” I say.

“It’s not your fault,” Leigh says, waving me off. “A few late nights at work won't kill me. At least it’s not Friday night she's asking me to stay late.”

“Why is Nicole so worried about this Warner

Group meeting? They're lawyers, right?"

Leigh shrugs. "Something like that. She's been unusually hush about it with me when I asked. Could be something juicy. Last time this happened, we acquired a major competitor's beauty supply business. Merged it with ours. Well, I say *merged*, but most of them were fired eventually. It's a dog-eat-dog world out there."

I nod, understanding Nicole's true nature. Leigh leaves and for a change, I get my work done to leave on time. I leave my office and wish Leigh a goodnight.

She's stuffing some beauty supplies into a large suitcase, when she stops and smiles at me. "This must look bad," she says. "Nicole lets me try samples of our supplies at home in exchange for my feedback."

"Well, you're a good test subject for them." I laugh. "See you tomorrow."

Leigh waves at me as I head along the hallway and take the elevator down with several colleagues. The big talk is the Warner Group meeting tomorrow. It seems like it's all that's been talked about all day and most of the week.

I walk to the parking lot, thinking about how I'm going to tell Evan about what Nicole is doing. I still have no answers beside the complete truth.

My boss is blackmailing me with a promotion to sleep with you. Well, go on a date, as she put it. Reminisce about their old flame, on our anniversary. The idea of it still bothers me.

Did she somehow know today was our special day?

When I get to my car, I open the door and throw my purse inside. Before I close the door, a large scratch across the driver's side door catches my attention. I stand back and notice the scratch goes straight across the entire side of my vehicle.

Someone keyed my car.

Before I completely lose it, I notice something worse. My driver's side tire has been slashed as well.

I look around the parking lot as if trying to find the culprit still hanging around. I know this area isn't the best, but this is beyond what would be expected. I look at the few cars in the lot, which are perfectly fine. No scratches. No slashed tires except my vehicle.

I think of Nicole. She doesn't come off like a woman who would key my car, but then again she didn't seem like someone who would blackmail me either.

How cliche. An ex-girlfriend slashing tires.

I sigh. This can't be her.

I call Evan. I'll need his help to put the spare on. When he doesn't pick up, I text him.

I open the trunk and look for where the spare is kept. After some time, I find it, but I've never changed a tire before. I think about just calling a tow company for help.

I google the restaurant we have reservations

at, click on the number and call. A man picks up the phone immediately.

"La Brezza restaurant. How can I help you?" he says.

"Yes, hi," I say. "I have reservations today."

"What's the name?"

"Walker. Alice Walker. I made reservations for two. I think my husband may be there, but I can't reach him. I was hoping you could let him know I'll be late." I think of the tire. "Well, maybe I should just speak with him. Can you ask him to call me please?"

The man doesn't respond for a moment. "Are you wanting to add an extra person to your reservation tonight?" he asks. "I'm sorry, but we're fully booked. I won't be able to accommodate this for you. Perhaps a different night I could."

I know this restaurant is busy. Leigh told me you have to book at least a week in advance to get in, and it's usually packed.

"No," I say. "I'm just running late." I can't have Evan come to me and put on my spare tire. If I do, I'll lose the reservation. The only thing I had to look forward to tonight was a fancy dinner. "Can you just let my husband know I'm on my way? I have a flat tire, but you're not too far away. I can take a taxi." I start looking around the street and spot one coming across an intersection.

"I'm sorry, miss, but I'm not able to add an extra person to your table," the man says. "We're fully booked tonight."

"What do you mean? The reservation is for two."

The man pauses again. "That's right, and there are two people sitting at the table now."

CHAPTER 21

Nicole

I watch Evan from across the restaurant, not wanting him to see me, not right away at least.

He's just as handsome as ever.

I bet Alice and him would have had an amazing anniversary dinner had I not interrupted their day. I smile.

Evan could really shine when I was with him, and many of those days were on special occasions, like anniversaries. He enjoyed romancing me on days like this. He would ramp up everything. The flirting was sexier. The sex was amazing. Everything about him was perfect.

Alice must have a similar experience. She's likely already had several from their years together. Tonight is going to be different.

It's time for me to reminisce.

I'm dressed to kill as well. In our time together, he gushed whenever I wore bright red. I have on a slimming red dress. The slit up my dress reveals my toned legs. I know he'll love it.

I saunter to his table, immediately catching

his attention. I see the shock in his face first, followed by his stare that examined my body, my dress and figure. I know I have him just where I want him already, just from that look. Just as I had when he was mine.

Whether he wants to admit it or not, I'll get what I want.

"What are you doing here?" he says softly, not wanting to cause a scene.

I sit in the empty chair across from him, and grin. I fix my dress as I stare at him wide-eyed. "I used to love it when you took me to places like this," I say.

"Don't sit down," he says, gritting his teeth. "I told you to leave me alone."

"You say a lot of things, Evan." I smile wider. "You told me something different at the bar last week."

"That was a mistake," he says, lowering his head. "I left that night. I told you to stop calling me. To leave Alice out of this." His eyes widen. "Where is she?"

"Your darling wife?" I ask playfully. "She's stuck at work, but I'm sure she'll be coming soon."

"What we had was years ago," he says, taking a sip of wine and looking around the room. He leans forward, taking in a deep breath. "It's over. So get over it. Leave me alone."

"Don't threaten me," I say slightly, raising my voice back. This was something we were good at back in the day. We would argue. Raise our voices and screw our rage away after. “Does she know anything about you? Does she know anything about us? Why we broke up? Did you bother to tell her?” I laugh, knowing the answer. “Don't threaten me, or I’ll have no other choice than to tell her everything.”

He takes a deep breath. “I told you, I don't care if you do. You won't have power over me or Alice. She’ll quit.”

“Is she better than me?” I ask, changing the subject. “Your boring wife. Does she get your blood boiling like I did? Did she keep your interest as much as me? Is she better in bed?”

Evan turns his head and looks like he’s seen a ghost. I turn and see Alice, storming towards us. If looks could kill, I’d have been dead as soon as she entered the restaurant.

“What are you doing?” she asks, staring at me.

I roll my eyes. “Alice. What took you so long? Join us.”

She stares at her husband. “Why is she here?”

Evan turns to Alice. “She’s leaving. She’s leaving for good.” He looks now at me, full of rage. “And so is Alice. She’s quitting today. Find someone else to torment, Nicole.”

I look around the room and notice a few stares at us. I’m not one for attention seeking in that way. "I said sit," I repeat. I look over at the table beside me where a table of three are eating peacefully. "I'm sorry, are you using this chair?" Before they answer me, I stand up, grab it and put it between Evan and me. I gesture for Alice to sit.

"Evan," I say calmly. "Please, ask your wife to sit with us. Or else."

He looks at Alice and at me for a few moments, before asking her to.

"This is crazy," Alice says. She looks at me intensely, slowly sitting down. "Why are you doing this to us? Evan doesn't want to be with you anymore. He's my husband."

I smile. "Ten thousand dollars."

"What?" Alice says, shocked.

Evan takes a sip of wine, trying to calm himself.

"Ten thousand dollars. That's what I'm willing to pay."

CHAPTER 22

Alice

I stare at her blankly, my breath paused. Looking beside me, I see my husband thankfully has a similar face.

Is she really asking what I think she is?

"Fine, Alice," Nicole says, sighing. "Let's make it twenty." She stares at Evan. "All for one night's work. It will be the most you could ever make, Evan." She smirks at my husband wickedly.

Evan's rageful eyes intensify as he grips the side of the table. "Just leave us alone. You're just as crazy as you were when we were younger."

Nicole's smile fades. "Don't ever call me that. Not after what happened. You don't get to say that to me, ever! Remember that."

I'm still attempting to catch my breath but feel like my face will turn blue. I'm light-headed and could faint. Maybe it would be better if I did. I could wake up to a situation that made more sense than what was happening.

Nicole laughs. "Alice, you're a better negotiator than I thought you would be... Fifty thousand dollars. Final amount." She grins at Evan. "Payable after services rendered."

"Let's get the hell out of here," Evan says, tossing his napkin on the table. "I'm not going to listen to this any further."

Nicole stares at me intensely again. "She'll be fired. She won't be able to work anywhere, not as an executive again. I remember during our interview, you talked so much about how you wanted to be, well, like me someday. You even told me that the other day."

"That was... before," I say, finally managing to find words. "Before finding out who you were."

She laughs. "You don't know anything about me." Her happy aura fades when she turns to look at Evan. "In fact, you don't even know much about him either, do you?"

"What do you mean?" I say, confused. I glance at Evan, who looks deflated in his chair, and back at Nicole. "What does that mean?" I repeat.

Nicole gazes around the room. "Please, don't make a scene. This is a fancy restaurant, after all, Alice." She looks at Evan. "Well, for one, he's gambling again."

Evan seems surprised.

"How do you know that?" he asks, confused.

She laughs again. "I know you, Evan. I know you. As soon as you hooked up with your brother, I knew you two were going to find trouble. Find a table somewhere. One time, Evan spent over ten thousand one night on blackjack. I nearly lost it with him. For one thing, he never made money. For another, your brother, Tommy, always pushed you to spend more."

I'm holding my breath again and release it, letting out a gust of air.

I stare at Evan. "You told me you would never go again. Did you go to a casino?" When Evan doesn't respond, I think of what he said about materials he paid for the house renovations. "The money you had for the house. Did you spend it? How much? How much did you gamble?"

Evan doesn't answer. He glances back up at Nicole. "How did you know?"

Nicole gives me a comforting look. "Something tells me, Alice, that it was likely all of it. Just like finding a job, Evan wasn't ever good at the felt tables either."

My eyes widen. I trusted him with the renovations. He told me he paid a bunch for materials, and I assumed he did. I didn't ask for receipts.

"Tell her about the bar, too," Nicole says. She looks over at the nearest table. An elderly couple is enjoying their pasta, unaware of the life-shattering moments I'm having.

I look at Evan. "What did you do?"

Evan lowers his head again. "Stop, please."

"Oh, I could go on, and on, and on," Nicole says with a devilish smirk. She looks at me. "There's a lot to know about Evan. He's not the proper husband who you think he is. He has skeletons in his closet. More than gambling debts."

"Stop," Evan says, slightly raising his voice.

A waiter comes to the table. "Would you like a menu?" he asks.

Nicole answers for me. "Maybe a bottle of your finest red, please, to start. Thank you." The waiter smiles and leaves. Nicole turns back to us. I can almost feel how powerful she must feel over both of us. My husband is strong-willed, boisterous. I look at him now, and he seems weak. He looks so frail that if he was standing, he would crumble to the floor attempting to take a step, and it's all because of Nicole Barrett.

What else does she have on him? How did she know about Evan going to the casino if he hadn't told her?

It hits me.

"You've been following us, haven't you?" I ask her.

Nicole looks at me, confused. "I don't have to follow you to know what you're doing."

"The phone calls, that person outside our window last week." I look at Nicole. "That was you, wasn't it?"

She sighs. "We're getting way off track now. I came here to make you an offer of a lifetime. Fifty thousand. One night." She points out the large window. "I'm in the tallest building, right there. Top floor. It's the most luxurious building in Toronto. Evan meets me at my building. Ten at night on Friday, sharp. We reminisce." She smiles at Evan. She looks back at me. "And you get what you want, Alice. That VP position, it's yours. I'll announce it on Monday for everyone to know."

I stare at my husband, unsure what to say or think. "You want Evan that badly that you'll do all of this? Why?"

"Reminisce. I told you," she says. "Evan has a certain skill, a way of comforting people when they need it. I need it right now. If I get what I want, you'll get what you want. A top executive position. Stay with the LBS as long as it takes to leverage what you need to get a president's job somewhere else. A glowing recommendation from me to go along with it... You won't even have to move offices Alice; you're already in the VP's chair. It's yours if you're willing. And Evan gets to pay back his debt. It's a win, win, win, situation." She grins.

"You knew who I was before you hired me," I state, knowing the truth. "You've been following me. Calling me."

"I don't know about any of that," she says. "What I do know is if I get what I want, I'll back off. Leave you alone. It'll be like I've disappeared from your personal life entirely."

"Promise?" Evan says at a whisper.

"I'm a woman of my word," she says confidently.

"We can't do this," I say. "This is outrageous."

"Ten on Friday, at my place," Nicole repeats. "If Evan is there, I'll have my answer. If he's not, I'll know. I won't speak about it again to you, Alice. I wouldn't want you to record my words." She laughs.

I shake my head. "Damn you."

She looks at me sternly. "Someday, when you look back at this, you'll thank me for the life that you have. Your lifestyle. Your mansion. Your beautiful car. Your future kids' upper-class lifestyle, carefree. It will all be because of this decision. They won't have to live in squalor like you, Alice. They don't need the life that you grew up in." She gives me a concerning look, arching an eyebrow. "They can have better, and so can you. But, if he's not at my place, I'll make your lives absolute hell. If you try to screw with me and go public with this, I'll ruin you completely." She looks at me. "You won't be able to get a job as a supervisor at a fast-food restaurant anywhere in North America."

The waiter comes, a bottle of red wine in his hand. Nicole smiles at him. "Chateau Nigril, 2005," he says.

Nicole thanks him as he pours three glasses of wine before leaving. Evan and I watch Nicole as she takes her glass and raises it to us.

"And happy anniversary."

CHAPTER 23

"Twenty thousand dollars," I repeat. Evan paces around our living room, in our house that we can't afford. "Evan!" I shout. "You gambled away twenty grand? How could you— how did this happen?"

"When we got back to Ontario, I started seeing Tommy more and more. He wanted to go out for a little blackjack, like we used to. Like the old times. He didn't know I had problems with it. I never told my family."

I nod. That part made sense. I knew all of that. He felt a lot of shame after he racked up ten thousand in debt. We had a lot of problems in our relationship at that time too. He promised he wouldn't go again. We came up with a payment plan with the bank to pay back the money he spent from his line of credit. It irked me back then that the money was for school. He was supposed to use that money to get enrolled into a Bachelor of Education degree and become a teacher. That was its purpose. Instead, he spent it on cards, making nothing. Losing everything.

He never went to school. He had no money. And as his girlfriend, I wasn't willing to give him any help. We put off getting married because of it. I needed him to show me that he meant what he said. He needed to show that he could pay off the debt and stop gambling.

That was the longest I had seen him work.

Eventually he paid it off, and things were better, until now.

"I know all of that," I tell Evan. "So this is Tommy's fault?"

He shakes his head. "It's not. He didn't know. He didn't know what happened. I didn't tell him. I thought a little game would be okay, and I was surprised when we went and I felt in control of my urges to spend more. Within an hour, I was up a thousand from when I walked in the door."

I take a deep breath, knowing what's about to come out of his mouth. "And of course," I say, beating him to it, "you didn't leave and lost it all."

He shakes his head. "No, I did leave. I bought Tommy lunch at a steakhouse. We went back to the house and worked all night on the renos." He laughs. "Then I started going by myself. We got into a fight about it. He saw what I was like at the tables the next day when I demanded we go back. I was almost hypnotized. Right away, I started losing. Within an hour, I was down almost three thousand, losing two from my pocket and the one I made the day before."

"Two thousand of our money," I repeat. "Our money, no, my money. You haven't been working, Evan."

He put out a hand, pleading with me to let him finish. "And then I made that money back, but I was even. Tommy wanted to leave. We got into a fight. He left. I stayed. I stayed for a while. I started losing more, and more. Just like last time, I thought I could catch up. Get back to where I started, at the minimum. I didn't. It was all gone. When I went to your office last week, I wanted to tell you. I chose not to. You were having a bad day."

"Don't blame this on me!" I shout.

"No, you're right. I should have said something. I was scared of what you would say. Then I saw Nicole. I nearly died when I saw her. It was a blast from the past. Then I realized she was your boss. I hated that, but there wasn't much I could do. I went to the bar that night, thinking about how I was ever going to tell you about what I did. How I lost our— your money." He lowers his head, taking in a deep breath. "I didn't know how to. I was scared to. Scared you would leave me, like you said you would after it happened last time. We weren't married then, but, if it was me, I would have left. I was lucky you stayed with me. Despite what a piece of shit I was, you did. This time, I'm not sure if you would— will."

I lower my head. When I look up, his bright brown eyes are staring at me, examining me to see if I'm about to burst out in anger or tears. "I understand why you didn't want to tell me, but we're married. We're supposed to be a team. You can't lie to me, or continue to lie."

"I should have told you sooner."

"Why did you reach out to Nicole and meet her at the bar? You came back late that night. What did you do?"

"I didn't reach out to Nicole. She was just there, at the bar. I'm not sure when she got there. I had a few beers, and she came and sat beside me. She said she was there with someone else and spotted me. Out of desperation, I asked her for money. A loan. Something I could pay back for what I spent. Not gamble it. To make it right. She said yes, but with a condition, and that condition, you already have an idea what it is."

"To have you again."

Evan nods. "I got angry. I left. She started calling me. I hung up on her a few times."

"I think she's calling me too," I say. "She's been breathing into the phone." I remember a time in the office when Nicole was near me, and someone called and breathed into the phone. So, if it is Nicole who's calling me, who was it that time? "Or maybe it's not her, but someone else. Someone she's getting to call me."

He breathes in deep. "She hasn't done that to me. She's always very straightforward, telling me to meet with her to discuss a loan. I knew

I made a mistake that night in the bar even talking to a person like Nicole again. She's terrible. Manipulative. Vindictive."

"What do we do?" I ask.

"I don't know. I'm sorry."

I sit on the couch and rub my face, wishing I could wake up from this nightmare. "She knew who I was when she hired me. That person outside our house. I think that was her too."

"Maybe not," Evan says. "I don't think she would go that far. Then again, after what happened tonight, I'm starting to change my mind. She was always off, but this is different."

I raise my head. "We could… sell the house and move back to Vancouver. I could get my old job back. We would be in debt, from moving twice, realtor fees, and what you gambled." I shake my head. "But we could figure it out. You work again, and I mean it."

"Of course," he says. "I will do what I need to do to make this right."

How stupid am I to think my husband will ever be anything but what he is? A person who would go behind my back and gamble our savings.

"You're going to have a separate account," I say. "An allowance, so you can't spend more than what you make. No credit cards in your name ever again. I mean it, Evan." It was something we talked about last time this happened, and Evan did well when he did. It was only when I began to trust him and not worry that things got worse. “No more joint credit or bank account. It’s back to how it was before.”

He nods. “Of course. Whatever I need to do. Just don't leave.”

I sigh. “I’ll talk to my old boss tomorrow morning.” I stare at Evan. “You still have that real estate lady's phone number? The one who worked with us on buying this house?”

“I do,” he says.

“Good. Talk to her. Figure out how long it would take to get this house back on the market and what price we could sell for.” I think of the shadowy person outside our house last week. “Just call her. Don’t have her come by. We can't risk it if Nicole is watching us.”

Evan sighs. “I know Nicole. If we don't do what she wants, she’ll make it hard for you to ever get a good job again. If we move back to Vancouver, the best you may ever do is your old job, maybe work up the chain there, but you were pretty close to the top already.”

I sigh. “My whole career is going to end because of you.” I look at my husband, unable to hide my rage. “It’s what you always wanted, me giving up my dream. Meanwhile you don't ever work a day in your life. You stay home... and do what? Not renovations! Gamble my money.”

Evan lowers his head and sits on the couch. “I don't know what to say. I should just shut up.” He takes in a breath. “I could just… do it.”

“You mean, meet with Nicole?’ I can feel my blood pressure rising. “You… you should shut up,” I agree.

He puts his hands up. “I don't know what to do.”

I try to collect myself. Nicole being who she is isn’t Evan's fault, I remind myself. She is the one who is doing this to us. Evan gambled, yes, but that's not Nicole's fault. I’m mad at both my husband and his ex-fiancé. Both are causing me unreal amounts of stress. I almost want to stand up and shout that they deserve each other and storm off.

Instead, I sit and think. It's hard to come up with a plan that doesn't end with my career ruined, settling in Vancouver, or ending in divorce. I told myself in the past if he was to ever get out of hand with his gambling, I wouldn't stay with him. He has been so good for years. He moves back to Ontario, and hangs out with his brother, and already he's back to his old ways.

It wasn't Tommy's fault, he tells me. It's hard not to hate both the Walker brothers in the moment.

“What do we do?” I repeat Evan’s words.

“I like what you said. We can go back to Vancouver. Sell this house. I’ll work. I won't be stupid either. I’ll do everything that's expected. We get away from Nicole, far away.”

And by doing so, I'll give up my dream of what I wanted since I was a little girl.

I remember what Nicole said at the restaurant tonight. "What else does she have on you?" I ask him. "You have skeletons in your closet. You need to tell me everything, now."

He looks down. "She's just trying to get in our heads even more. She's trying to put us against each other. That's how she is. That's how she always is. The woman is vindictive."

I stand up from the couch, my hands at the side of my head, rubbing a headache I don't actually have. Even though I don't, I feel like my head could explode at any moment. I start walking up the stairs slowly without saying a word to my husband.

"Where are you going?" he asks.

"Bed. I can't do this anymore tonight. I need rest." Evan starts to follow me, until I put a firm hand on his chest. "Sleep on the couch tonight."

CHAPTER 24

"I'm sorry, Alice. We can't take you back," my old boss, Harold Lirewood, says. His voice sounds old and brittle, just as he looked in real life. Even though I hate his answer, just hearing his voice comforts me in a weird way. I want to tell him all the terrible things that've happened, but why would he care? I was just his employee. He wasn't my parent. "I'm so sorry, Alice," he repeats. "I had hoped you would prefer it out there. The new man we hired to take your job, he's been doing so well. And, let's be honest, even if we hired you back, I know you wouldn't be happy in the position. You would leave again. And where would that put us? Having to go through this process again. That would be too much."

I lower my head, and lean against the hallway wall. "I understand, Mr. Lirewood."

"No hard feelings though, right?" he asks.

I take in a deep breath. Working for him was a dream compared to being at Lovely Beauty Supplies. "None whatsoever," I answer.

"You take care of yourself, Alice," he says. His

old voice is having difficulty completing his words. I wonder if he's as emotional as I am right now.

"Wait, Mr. Lirewood," I say quickly before he ends the call. "I just wanted to say thanks. I had some great times working for you. Thank you for being amazing to work for."

There's a pause on the phone, and I can almost see the old man smile as if I'm in the room with him. It was always something very endearing about his presence.

"Well, we loved having you," he says. "But I know you'll do great things in Toronto. Better than what I could ever give you. I joked with our staff after you left that someday we'd read about you in magazines or news articles because of how successful you'll become. My hope is that you remember the little guy you worked for before and mention us." He laughs. "I know that you're destined to do great things." I feel my stomach in knots when he says the words. "Goodbye."

"Bye, Mr. Lirewood." We end the call, and I raise my head, looking around me. People walk past me, but none of them I know. I snuck onto a different floor than the thirtieth, where LBS is. I needed a little privacy for my calls and couldn't risk Nicole hearing them.

I dial Evan and he immediately picks up. "My old job isn't available to me now," I say as soon as he answers, getting to the point.

"Shit," he says under his breath. "I thought

the old man would take you back in an instant."

I think of my old boss's face, the smile he would brandish whenever I did good work and he was happy. I loved the satisfaction it gave me, but I really loved doing it for him.

I thought of my father. He never smiled. He never gave me the time of day. He was never happy with me.

"He's not wrong for not taking me back," I say. "He knows me. He knows I want better." I sigh. "I should have never left."

I could have found work eventually. Mr. Lirewood had hired his adult children for the top positions, though. They were going to take over for him when he passed. I was at the top of my old company. There was nowhere else to go in that job. I had to leave to do better.

"Did you call the real estate agent?" I ask. I half expect him to tell me he hasn't, knowing him, but he surprises me when he says he has. "And what did she say?"

"Well, of course she would be happy to represent us in the sale. I told her we were in the middle of some renovations. She said we would have to finish the paint job and the tiles in the bathroom before we could put it on the market."

I sigh. Why did he and Tommy have to take on so much at once with the renos?

"How much?" I ask. "How much more money do you need to finish what you have?"

"A few thousand," he says. "Worst case, I could ask Tommy."

I nod even though he's not in the room. "You should just ask him. Maybe don't tell him everything that's happening with you-know-who."

"I can't even get a hold of him. He hasn't called me back. He's on summer vacation from the school. What could the guy even be doing?"

"What about the price for the house?" I ask. "What did the real estate agent say?"

There's a bit of a pause. "Not much better than what we got it for, or even less. In the past few months, interest rates have kept climbing and aren't expected to go down. It's a fixer-upper in a nice area, yes, but many people are moving out of Toronto. She told me we have the most expensive real estate in the world."

I put a hand to my forehead. It's the worst news I can imagine. After what we have to pay the real estate agent in fees and all the other costs of selling a house, we could be tens of thousands in debt. I won't even have enough for a down payment on a house in Vancouver. We'll be back to renting and completely broke.

"I've got to go," I say.

"Wait, Alice," he says quickly. I sigh and wait for him to say whatever he has on his mind. "I can come by and pick you up if you want."

"Pick me up?"

"Why stay there? Let's just leave, now. Pack

up your office and go."

"I have to get off the phone. I have to go back to my floor." I end the call, and head back to the elevator. Once on the company floor, I pass Leigh at reception, who's on the phone. She waves at me when I walk past her. I give a thin smile back.

I look into Nicole's office. Two men in expensive suites are watching her give some kind of presentation. One of them laughs. Nicole nods as she points at a bar graph. The men stand up and both shake her hand.

I open my glass office door but listen in to their conversation as I leave.

"We'll be in touch, Ms. Barrett," the man in a navy suit says.

"Take care," she says, shaking both their hands again. "We'll have lunch soon."

I enter my office and sit at my desk, and watch Nicole in hers. After the men leave, she starts taking down some of the presentation information and takes a brief moment to look at me before sitting at her desk and typing at her computer.

I could do what she does. I know it.

I could have been a president of a company. The top executive.

I would have been great at it too. What would it have taken for me to be a woman like Nicole?

Stupid. Girl.

I get his words out of my mind. My father's

been dead over a year, and yet his words still haunt me. He haunts me.

We're going to be broke for years to come. It's going to take a long time to get back to where we should be, even if Evan actually finds work, and somehow keeps it. A few nights ago, he mentioned having a child with me again. I shrugged him off, saying I needed to focus on my career right now. Lovely Beauty Supplies was my big break.

More like a big bust.

Even if I wanted to have a baby right now, how could I bring a child into this world with my life in shambles? We can't afford a decent place for a baby to live. We couldn't provide nice things to give it. I think of my house growing up. I was lucky if my parents ever bought a toy for me. I remember walking down an alley when I was a child, coming home from school. I found a beat-up looking Barbie sticking out of a garbage bag in a bin behind a house. I grabbed it quickly while seeing if anyone was around. I played with that doll with one eye for years.

My child was going to get better.

Stupid. Girl.

I cringe at the thought of him. I won't let my baby be raised like I was. I was going to give it the best I never had.

I sigh when I notice my finger is already checking my pulse even though I didn't realize I had it there.

A knock on my glass door makes same jump. Leigh grins from outside and comes in.

"Hey, girly," she says playfully. "I'm depressed." She mocks a frown. "No coffee date with you for a few days now. Are you ignoring me?" She laughs.

"No, sorry," I say. "Things have been busy."

"Sorry, I'll leave," she says. "I know how hard your job is. I just wanted to come in and say hi." She turns to leave but I call out to her, and she looks back at me.

I stand up from my desk and walk over. I can't hide the tear forming in my eye.

"Are you okay?" she asks. "What's wrong?"

I shake my head. Nicole must be watching. "I'm fine. I just want to thank you."

"For what?"

"You've been great. I really needed a friend out here, and I appreciate how nice you've been."

She laughs. "Stop it," she says, waving me off. "I love our coffee dates. I actually look forward to them. A lot of the people here never talk to me. I'm just the receptionist."

I sigh. "Well, rain check on coffee?"

"Are you sure everything's okay?" she asks. I nod and give a thin smile before she leaves.

I turn and see Nicole standing up in her office, facing me. For a brief moment, the two of us are squared off, the glass wall the only thing between us. She has a smirk on her face.

I sit at my desk and continue to work until it's time to leave. I go through the motions of saying goodbye to Leigh. She's getting ready to leave herself and is wearing her long scarf and hat, and reaches out for her large suitcase. She almost looks like a movie star. I like to dress well but Leigh takes it to another level. Usually, I would comment on her outfit, but today I have too many other thoughts running through my mind.

Then I spot her, my boss, the reason I can't think straight, standing in her office.

Nicole leaves her office and smiles at me. "Have a great night, Alice," she calls out.

I ignore her. I leave the building. I go to the parking lot. Enter my car. Drive home. The whole time I'm thinking of what I should do next.

Evan sees my car from the front window. He opens the door, looking concerned.

He gazes at me, waiting for an embrace, but I don't give him one. All I want to do is shake him, screaming as hard as I can. I brush past my husband as I walk into my house. I spot paint cans on the floor. One is open, and the smell of fresh paint hits my nostrils.

"I've been working all day," Evan says, closing the front door behind him. "I think I can get the house ready by the end of the weekend. I'll put in the hours all day and night until it's done. Tommy still hasn't called me back, but that's okay. I can finish without his help. I—"

I turn to him. My emotionless face stops him in his tracks. “Friday with Nicole,” I say, staring at him. “I want you to… just do it.”

“What?” he says confused. “We can—”

I shake my head. “Do it. Go to her apartment.” I walk up the stairs, towards the bedroom, not looking back at my husband.

CHAPTER 25

Nicole

Today's meeting with the company's lawyers went well. It was something I had been dreading all week.

I thought for sure my stakeholder meeting with them would bring up that they knew what I've been up to.

They would know how much money I've embezzled from Lovely Beauty Supplies. I've been taking money from them for some time now.

It was stupid. I needed more capital to cover my losses from some bad investments. I could pay it back eventually, but the lawyers began sniffing around. I started getting emails asking questions.

It got to the point where our top accountant called me about discrepancies. Discrepancies in funds that were missing that I couldn't explain sufficiently. The police were going to be called, he warned. I felt I was already caught.

I knew my time was coming to an end. The writing was on the wall.

It was a white-collar crime, though. I hadn't

murdered someone. I would be in prison for a few years max. Maybe out after a year for good behaviour.

Then today's meeting happened, and for a change I felt confident that maybe things will work out.

There's no way to put back the money that I took. Even if I give up all my assets, it wouldn't make up for it.

I fudged the numbers with my own accounting team to try and make things look better. Perhaps that worked. My investors could be thinking things are fine. The missing money could be explained by the bullshit I put together at my presentation.

I sigh. Sometimes people do strange things when they think their life is about to end. I was willing to hire someone like Alice just to have Evan back in my life again.

I sit in my office and stare at the empty vice president's room beside mine.

Fifty thousand dollars. I nearly laugh out loud. As if I have that kind of money to give. I certainly wouldn't spend that for Evan.

The office is empty. Alice left for the day without a word to me. Today was not the day to not know what the Walkers were doing.

The last thing I wanted to hear would be the police showing up at their house and them telling them everything that's happened.

I pick up my phone and dial her number. For a moment, I'm startled when I hear a phone ringing from outside my office.

I see Leigh standing outside my room. I look at her strangely as she enters.

"What are you doing here?" I ask. "You're supposed to be watching Alice. I told you to—"

"I'm not doing this anymore," she interrupts.

I put a hand to my chest, not understanding this blatant insubordination.

"This is the last night," I say, but then correct myself. "Well, tomorrow night too, actually. Then you're done."

"No," she says curtly. "You had me watch Alice the past week. I did what you asked without asking questions. I do a lot of things for you without questions."

"That's why I made you my executive assistant!" I shout.

"I'm just the receptionist still," she cuts me off. "You never hired another receptionist."

"Things are busy, Leigh. You know that. I—"

"You had enough time to hire Alice," she says back. "But not enough to follow through with what you promised me. I was to have my own office! My own business cards."

"I'm working on that, Leigh," I say, putting my hands up. "Just go to her house tonight. Last time. I need you."

"No," she says again. "I've been following her and her husband. I had to watch him at the casino for you. You even had me call Alice and breathe into the phone like a maniac. What's your problem with her?"

"That's between her and me," I say. I stand up from my desk and get closer to Leigh. "Now, this is almost over. Just do what I say. If you don't, you won't get any of the bonuses I said."

"Ten thousand?" she says with a laugh. "I'm getting the subtle hint that I won't be getting a dime from you, ever."

"You will," I say, raising my voice. "Just do what I ask, and you will."

"Just like the office you promised me," she says, pacing.

"I'll raise it to fifteen thousand," I say. "Just finish what you started. I'm not asking you to hurt anyone."

"Just stalk them," she says. "I can't believe I did this. It's over. I'm done. And if you try anything, I'll call the cops and tell them everything. I'll tell Alice everything." She folds her arms. "I should tell her everything. She's honestly such a nice person. I can't believe I've done these things to her. And for what? A little money that you won't even pay up."

"Leigh!" I call out as she storms out of my office. I follow her until we're near her reception area. She grabs the large case near her desk.

"No," she says again, this time with a smile.

"You know, I love saying no to you. I should have said it a long time ago."

"I'll tell the cops about your stealing!" I say.

She stops in her tracks. "What?"

"I know how much product you've taken over the past few years. You put it in that large suitcase. It looks like you're boarding an airplane for a long trip every time I see you." I scoff. "What, it must be over ten thousand dollars' worth of items by now, and that's at production price. Imagine I tell the police how much the retail price of what you've taken is. In Canada, theft over five thousand can land you ten years in prison!"

She rolls her eyes at me and shuffles her blond hair over her shoulder. "You told me I could take some. You said I was basically your personal product tester."

"Right, but I never said you could buy the largest bag I've ever seen and ransack the place once a week."

She breathes in deep. She bends down and opens the side of the case. She digs her hand inside, grabbing a bottle of LBS's new shampoo line. She throws it towards me.

"Take it back, then!" she yells. She takes more items and throws them at my feet. "Take it all back. I quit!" She turns and walks away from me, leaving her bag behind.

"No!" I say to her, but she doesn't turn to acknowledge me. "You're fired!"

CHAPTER 26

Alice

I walk onto the thirtieth floor of LBS. I'll try not to scream at Nicole if I see her, but right away I look into her office and can see her at her desk, fidgeting with papers.

I want to storm in there and yell at her to leave me alone. Instead, I continue toward my own office.

I walk past reception, but for a change Leigh isn't there. I don't see a fancy coffee cup or her large luggage beside her desk.

I glimpse at the bold words written at the bottom of the reception desk. Have A Beautiful Day.

I cringe, but shake it off as I enter my glass prison of an office.

Before I start another day in this hell, Nicole is at my door and entering. This time, she doesn't knock but brazenly walks inside.

What strikes me as different is how terrible she looks. Her dolled-up blond hair that's usually straightened and brushed to perfection is in a disheveled bun.

“I need to know your answer, now,” she says. “I need to know this instant.”

She doesn't even bother with a good morning or any of the niceties she’s used to faking with me. I actually appreciate her not playing with me today. I’m not sure how much more embarrassment I can take. I know I have no poker face and can only imagine how much anger I’m showing, staring at the woman who wants to steal my husband.

I take a deep breath, not faking a smile. I look at her as if she burped in front of me. “He’ll be there. Ten. Your place.” A grin spreads across her face. This time it's genuine. She’s getting what she wants from me. I better get what I deserve.

“Fifty grand,” she says. “I’ll have the money ready for you next week. Today, I need you to officially send me your resume for the position of vice president of Lovely Beauty Supplies.”

“Not a problem,” I say curtly. “I’ll have that ready for you right away.” I open my laptop and type in my password. I look up at her, that stupid smile still plastered on her face. “Is there anything else?”

“No, that will be everything,” she says. “I'm leaving. I’ll be working from home. You're in charge while I’m away. Is that fine?”

I pause. This was what I wanted, wasn't it? Now she’s saying the words after I’ve promised her my husband tonight. A bittersweet moment. I’m in charge of LBS today.

It's something I've always dreamed of. I thought if it ever happened to me, I'd feel overwhelmed with happiness and a sense of achievement.

Instead, I feel like I'll regurgitate over my entire glass office for everyone to see. Poor Steve the cleaner will hate me.

I nod in response. She doesn't poke me further, takes the hint and leaves my office without another word. As I pretend to read my emails, I glance over my shoulder and take in Nicole packing up her laptop and some paperwork. She leaves her office and passes the empty reception area.

I breathe out deeply.

What have I done?

What deal with a devil have I made?

I look at an email from late last night that catches my attention. "Staffing Announcement," the header reads. It's from Nicole. I click on it.

"Hello everyone,

Leigh Olson is no longer employed by or affiliated with Lovely Beauty Supplies.

Best regards,

Nicole Barrett."

Did she quit? Was she fired?

Leigh seemed so normal yesterday while at work. What happened?

I lower my head, wondering, until a knock on my office door makes me raise my head. Walt

Denellio, a supervisor in the customer service department, waves at me.

When he enters, I put on a fake smile for him. "Good morning, Walt."

"Morning, Alice," he says quickly. He points at Nicole's office. "Did she leave? I needed to go over a few things with her today."

I nod. "She's away for the rest of the day, but you can run it past me. She asked me to be in charge today."

He pauses. "Sounds good." He sits at the other side of my desk and spreads out some Excel sheets for me to see.

CHAPTER 27

When I park outside my house after a long day of work, the lights are all off. For a moment I worry Evan has already left, or worse, left me.

When I open the front door, though, he's sitting on the couch, staring at the television that's not on.

"I feel sick to my stomach," he says, not looking at me. "Rotten inside. I haven't been able to do anything all day." I can tell as much since he's still in jogging pants and a white shirt. He looks at me finally. "I'm not some kind of male escort. This won't be a thing I ever do again."

I lower my head. "I know. It won't be."

He shakes his head. "If she wants it to be, she'll find something to hang over our heads."

I nod. "Who cares if she does. If she doesn't pay, we'll go public. I don't need recordings of her talking about it. The building she's at likely has security cameras or a check-in procedure. It will show that you were there tonight. With me getting a quick promotion, everything will add up. If she doesn't pay, or give me what I want, she'll be ruined and she knows it. She has to follow through with this now."

He stands up in front of the couch and faces me. "And I have to as well? This isn't right. I'm your husband. This is our marriage. She can't control that. She never can. We still can say screw it. End this here, before everything changes."

I look away from him. "No." If I do, she wins. My career will be ruined. Our finances will be destroyed. In a few years of working crappy jobs and being heavily in debt from everything that's happened here, I know I'll resent Evan. I'll hate him for not doing this.

This was my dream. This position is all I ever wanted. I won't let Nicole take that away from me. I won't let Evan ruin this either with his gambling.

One night, and he makes everything right.

I think of them kissing and cringe.

I take in a deep breath. "Just, please, do this."

"If I do, you'll hate me forever for it," Evan says. "You already hate me now. Is our marriage already doomed? What's the point, then?"

I look up at him. "You do this, and not only will you fix what you've done wrong, but we'll never talk about this again. The moment I can find another executive job, I will leave LBS, and Nicole."

"She'll never leave us alone," he says.

I shake my head. "She will." If she doesn't, I don't like to think of what I'd do to her. I've never been a violent woman, but the thought of beating up Nicole in my office, the glass walls giving everyone a show of me kicking her ass, would be fantastic.

"Are we going to be okay?" Evan asks. It's a fair question. I've barely looked at him since yesterday. I haven't even kissed him.

"We will," I tell him, not knowing if I'm lying to myself now.

CHAPTER 28

Nicole

I'm going to prison.

There's no denying it now. That's my fate. The police could kick down my door tonight. It doesn't matter what the lawyers at Warner find out about my fraudulent activities now.

It's all over for me.

I may as well enjoy one last night with someone I cared about before the rest of my life is spent behind cold steel bars.

I stare at the night sky from outside my balcony. The drapes in the bedroom move gently in the wind. I have on a white bathrobe as I wait for my guest to arrive.

I stare down at the little specks of cars and things moving below. They seem so free down there. My palatial apartment seems to be getting smaller. Soon it will be replaced by a room that's less than ten by ten feet.

It's enough to make a woman go mad, knowing what's in store for me.

Evan coming tonight is actually the best thing

I could ever have. Besides getting away with what I've done, Evan comforting me one last time is exactly what I need.

When we were together, so many years ago, he had a strange way of making me feel better by just being beside me. We could be like oil and vinegar most days, but when I needed him, he was there.

He's here again tonight for me. Not exactly something he wanted to do, but they could have said no. They could have flat-out refused me. Quit.

I wonder how much of this is Evans' choice or Alice's.

Does it matter?

Not really. I need something before the rest of my best years are taken away. Before my name is dragged through every newspaper. I can already see the headlines. Nobody will remember me for the amazing things I've done. It will all be overshadowed by what happened.

What I did.

For one night, I can pretend things are how they were supposed to be. I'll have Evan.

As much as I love him still, I hate him equally. I wonder what life would have been like had Evan not lost control. Had I not lost our baby inside me.

The miscarriage was his fault. He knows it. If he wasn't so violent, we could have had a beautiful life together.

Two weeks after he proposed, two weeks after

the miscarriage, I left him. I know the only reason he asked me to marry him was because I was pregnant. That didn't matter to me at the time. I was happy, well, usually happy. We fought all the time, but that was us.

That was our normal relationship.

I like to think we were so terrible for each other that it only made sense that we were perfect together.

Then I lost the child. It was because of what he did.

I still get upset about it, even years later. When I lost the child, I lost the only chance I had at a happy life.

I ended it with Evan.

I wondered for years if that was the right decision. I felt it was until my looming prison sentence was over my head; now I'm not so sure.

Tonight's going to be my chance to see.

Before I can get too down on myself, I hear a tapping at my front door. I finish my drink and smile. I remove my robe when I enter my bedroom, revealing my black lingerie. It's lacy, just like he loved.

When I open the door, his back is turned to me for a moment. When he looks at me, immediately I know he's happy with my choice. He scans my body, and for a moment, I can see the look of lust he had when we were younger. He was a hungry wolf, and I was his willing prey.

I wave him to enter, and he does without saying a word.

"Drink?" I ask, and he shakes his head.

Evan looks around my apartment, taking in its beauty. I wonder what he's thinking. He must often wonder what his life would have been like had we still been together.

Evan looks at the camera in the dark hallway. It's facing him and a red light is blinking below it.

"Don't worry," I say. "It's recording, but I don't have anything in the bedroom."

Evan lowers his head and takes in a deep breath. I can see the inner demons fighting inside him. Evan was a principled man, though a confusing one. Cheating was never something he would do.

I suppose that's what makes this more fun.

Is it really cheating if he cares deeply for the person he's doing it with? Or does that make things more grey? Had it not been for what he did, we would have stayed together. Alice would never be in the picture.

Evan knows that.

I bring him to the living room area. Again, he takes a moment to take in the panoramic windows, showcasing downtown Toronto at night.

He finally speaks. "It's beautiful up here," he manages.

I sit on the couch and pat my hand beside me. He takes the hint and sits down, although not very close to me.

I take in a deep breath. I don't like playing games. He needs to be in this, or leave. I won't force a man to do this.

"Evan," I say, touching his thigh, "you don't have to stay. You can go if you want."

He shakes his head. "I'm doing this for my marriage, not for you."

I shake my head. "You don't mean that. You will never get an opportunity like this ever again. No strings. I'm not nothing to you either. You cared for me once, right?" He doesn't answer immediately.

"Then why did you leave me?" His hands are together and fidgeting in his lap.

I grab one of his sweaty hands and hold it tightly. "I couldn't stay after what you did, you know that. I always loved you."

He looks up at me. "I love Alice now."

I nod. "I know."

He makes a face. "All of this, what you're doing, is just for me to be with you tonight?"

"One night," I remind him. My hand on his thigh is starting to get higher up his leg. I can feel his muscles tighten.

Before I can say another word, he leans in close to my body. I breathe out, waiting for his lips to kiss mine, but they don't.

He stands up abruptly, reaching down with his hand for me to grab it. I take it, and he lifts me off the couch with ease. With our bodies close to one another, I can feel the tension between us rising.

"Let's go to the bedroom," he says, staring at me intensely. I lead him down the hall, past the blinking red light of the camera, and open my bedroom door. I look at the dimly lit room, and the curtains moving in the breeze.

"You're never going to leave us alone, are you?" he says in a whisper.

I turn to him, and the look of lust has vanished from his face. What's replaced it is one of anger and disgust. A look of rage.

"What?" I say.

"Alice," he says, keeping his gaze on me. "You will never give her what she wants. You will never leave me alone. This isn't just one night, is it? You want to ruin everything I have. You always did." He breathes out. "You will never be out of our life."

CHAPTER 29

Alice

I sit at my desk at LBS. I couldn't stay home while Evan was with Nicole. I paced around the living room, kitchen and bedroom, waiting for him to leave and go do what I demanded of him.

Right after he left, I did too. At first I thought I would leave to stop him. Tell him how stupid I was for even considering him doing this. Instead, I stayed behind in traffic, letting his car get further ahead of mine until he was out of sight.

I don't think he saw me. He's probably busy thinking about what's going to happen tonight.

I always wondered if married couples could pinpoint the exact moment they knew their marriage was officially over.

I thought that finding out about Evan's gambling debt would be ours for me, but it isn't.

It's Nicole. It's tonight.

I went to LBS and sat in my office chair, every so often looking outside my window towards the group of buildings.

In the tallest of them, Nicole lives. In one of

them my husband is with her.

I take my mind off what's happening in that building between my husband and my boss by focusing on my work. At least I try. I open my emails and stare blankly at them. I open up spreadsheets with information that I would typically dive into but all of it seems trivial.

Nothing made sense anymore.

Isn't this what I wanted?

I did what Nicole asked. I submitted my resume for her consideration. Only it wasn't consideration. It was part of our deal.

What am I doing?

I stand up from my desk and go to the employee bathroom, turning on every light I can in the dark office as I do.

I stand in front of the bathroom mirror and look at myself in the reflection.

A young me would look at myself and be in awe. You did this? You accomplished this? Wow. You showed everyone what you're really worth in this world. Your family was wrong about you. You're not worthless. You've proven them all wrong.

Father was wrong. You showed them.

I turn on the sink and splash water on my face, taking a towel and drying myself. I lean in closer to the mirror.

Why don't I feel so accomplished? Why don't I feel powerful? Why don't I feel like I've proven my worth?

I lower my head, and a red stain on the corner of the marble counter catches my attention. I take my damp paper towel and clean it. I take another look at my reflection, hating myself more and more.

No matter how much I clean up what's around me, I'm still dirty. After Evan sleeps with my boss to get me a promotion, I'll always feel this way.

I immediately leave the bathroom and go past my office and head directly into Nicole's. On top of her desk is my resume. I take it and nearly tear it up right there.

Instead, I look around.

I look at her chair and feel the fine quality of its leather. I touch the material for a few more moments before sitting in it. I put my hands on her desk and let my fingers slide across it.

This could be mine. I deserve it. I've earned it.

Will the one blemish of what I'm allowing to happen tonight ruin everything for me? If I get what I want, and Evan gets redemption for his debt, will we not be happier? Both of us get what we need.

I look outside Nicole's office into mine.

Being a vice president will change everything for my career. It will change everything for Evan and me. Executives make all the money.

The people who work for them make peanuts compared to Nicole's salary.

And all it will take is one night to get what I want. How hard will it be to forget one night?

I turn my leg and my foot catches the open bottom drawer of her desk. I peek inside and can see a bottle. I open the drawer fully to see a corked wine bottle. It's been opened and half downed already. I smirk, thinking about the dark red stain in the bathroom. How often does Nicole come here to drink alone?

I take out the bottle and, with all my might, pull on the cork until it's free. I don't bother with rummaging through the drawer to find a glass and drink directly from it. I wipe my mouth with my sleeve and smile.

I look down at the open drawer and something else catches my attention. A picture frame.

I take another long drink of wine and put the bottle on the desk, before reaching down and grabbing the frame. I stare at the picture. It's of a young Nicole, on a farm it looks like. A black outline of a corn on the cob is painted on the side of the light blue barn. I stare at the bold black letters below the corn image. "Brooks County, the Corn Capital of Canada."

I laugh, thinking how innocent Nicole looks in this picture. Her fake smile that I've seen her wear on her face since starting at LBS is not the same as this one.

Her happiness is genuine.

I'm about to put the picture back in the drawer when I see another one inside. This one I recognize all too well.

It's the one of me and Evan.

The picture that I thought the cleaner had thrown away was in her drawer the entire time.

I stand up from the desk. I look at Evan and I and the picture we took on our honeymoon.

What have I become? What have I let our marriage turn into?

Part of me wants to pour the remaining wine on the desk and light it on fire.

Instead, I grab my resume, and without hesitation, tear it down the middle. To be more dramatic, I tear it into several more strips before throwing it around Nicole's office.

I stare outside the window, at Nicole's building.

It's already too late, I know, but I have to clean up the mess I've made. No matter what's already happened between Evan and her, I need to stop it now.

I leave the building without paying much attention to the security guard calling out to me to have a good night. I quickly get to my car without fear of the dangers around me like before.

All I have in mind is one thing. Get to Nicole's apartment. She gave us her apartment number. I just have to find a way to get inside.

I park illegally in a spot immediately outside Nicole's building. The city can tow my car for all I care. I need to get inside as quickly as possible, and I do.

If I wasn't in such a rush, I would be taken back by the marble floors and the grand fireplace in the lobby. It's something like you would see in an expensive hotel.

I spot someone in a glass office, almost eerily reminiscent of mine. I know immediately they work for the building and try my best to fit in and walk towards the elevator. Every bit of me wants to run to it and hit the button.

When I finally do, and the up button is illuminated I feel slightly better. I have no clue what I'm going to say or do when I get to her apartment.

"Can I help you?" the man says, coming out from his office. I don't answer him immediately and pray the elevator door opens soon. It doesn't and the man repeats himself.

I turn to him and smile. "Yes, hi, I'm here to meet my friend, Nicole. Nicole Barrett. She lives on the top floor. She's expecting me."

The elevator door finally opens.

"Ms.," he calls out to me. "Visitors after eleven have to sign in with photo I.D. and we have to call Ms. Barrett before you leave the lobby. Please come back."

I quickly enter the elevator and hit the close button. “She’s expecting me. I must be going!” I shout. I see the man's confused face as the doors close.

I wait impatiently for the elevator to reach the top floor.

My phone vibrates and I quickly take it out and see it’s a text from an unknown number.

“This wasn’t part of the deal,” it reads. An image of a red, bruised arm is attached. I breathe in, wondering what’s happening.

I anxiously watch as the elevator display shows each floor we’re passing until we get to the very top and the doors open.

I immediately run into the hallway. There’s only two doors. I knock continuously on one and when I don't hear any noises from inside, I panic and strike on the other door furiously.

Evan opens the door, confused. “Alice,” he says, his mouth gaping open. “What are you doing?”

His hair is disheveled and forehead glistening with sweat. I can only imagine why he looks this way, and immediately tears form in my eyes.

“It was a mistake,” I say, pushing past him. “We should have never agreed to this.” I storm into Nicole’s apartment. “Nicole!” I shout. “This is over!”

Evan comes into the room, his hands at his side. “I don’t know what happened,” he says, struggling to find the words.

"What?" I ask. "Nicole! Come out. Put on clothes. Do whatever you have to."

Evan puts his hands out. "You have to stop screaming," he says calmly, in a tone of voice that scares me.

"Where is she?" I ask.

He lowers his head. He walks into the bedroom. I half expect to see Nicole splayed on the bed, satisfied with the outcome of her deal with me. Instead, she isn't there, and Evan keeps walking through a patio door out to the balcony.

He looks down.

I stand beside him and feel a chill from the wind. "Where is she?"

I look down and see a few people standing around in a semi circle. The streetlight shows red staining the sidewalk directly below.

CHAPTER 30

"What's happened?" I shout, looking down at the messy pile of crimson staining the cement.

Evan covers his mouth, not answering.

"What the hell happened?" I yell at him.

"She jumped!" he answers. "She killed herself."

"Oh no, no," I say, trying to catch my breath. I feel nearly lightheaded. Looking so far down, I feel like I was nearly falling myself.

Evan grabs my shoulder. "She did it to herself," he repeats.

My world is spinning. How did this happen?

"Why?" I finally manage to ask.

Evan puts a hand to his mouth again and walks back into the bedroom. He looks at a large portrait over the bed of Nicole sitting at her desk in the office.

"She was upset, I guess, I don't know." He paces around more until he stops and looks at me. "I refused to go through with it. I called her out. I knew this wouldn't be the end of what she had planned for you, for me... us. This was just the terrible beginning."

I hear the sounds of distant police sirens. No doubt where those emergency vehicles were going. What remains of Nicole's body is below us, splattered on the sidewalk.

"So," I say, getting to grips with the situation, "you reject her and you see her jump?"

He looks at me, confused. "Yes, that's right."

I breathe out. "So when did you do this?" I take out my cell phone and show him the photo Nicole sent me of her bruised arm. "You did this? You're not saying everything that happened. Why, Evan?"

"I didn't touch her!" he shouts. "I didn't."

"So, she did this to herself?"

He pauses and looks at me. "I don't know. After I rejected her, she slammed her bedroom door on me. I knocked on the door to get her to open up."

"Why didn't you just leave?"

"I was scared. About what was she going to do to us now that I'd refused. I wanted her to stop! Leave us alone, you know."

"Did you do this for us?" I ask, pointing out toward the balcony.

"I told you no!" he shouts. "I didn't push her or toss her off the balcony. She closed the door. When I opened it, she had already jumped."

"I thought you said you saw her jump?"

"I don't know. It all happened so fast. I thought I saw her on the balcony, screaming before she jumped." He paces around the room more. "Oh god, this looks bad. We should... just leave."

"What!" I shout. "We can't just go. The man in the lobby saw me and likely saw you too."

"That damn camera," he says. "Nicole has a camera in her own hallway."

The image of the bruised arm sticks with me. "I don't understand the picture she sent me. How could she have done this herself?"

"I don't know," Evan shouts again. He grabs me sternly. "I never wanted to come here tonight. I did it for you! For us! I should have said no to this stupid plan."

The sounds of the sirens are closer now, and I hear more coming. Very soon, the police will be here. I go out onto the balcony, and stare down at the flashing red and blue lights below and the much larger crowd around the scene.

"What do we do?" Evan shouts. "What do we do?"

I go back into the hallway and see the camera Evan mentioned. It's facing towards the front door and looking right at me. I breathe in deep, looking at the blinking red light below it.

CHAPTER 31

I sit in a small room with two brawny detectives who stare back at me, asking and re-asking questions about everything that's happened. They introduced themselves to me when I first entered this small room, but for the life of me I can't remember. All I can think about is what happened to Nicole, and what it means for Evan and me.

Evan isn't with me. I can only assume he's in a similar small room somewhere in the police station looking at similar detectives, answering the same questions. I wonder how truthful he's been.

I've told the police everything. Every aspect I could think of that led me to tonight, I told them. I explained how we moved, my job at Lovely Beauty Supplies. What Nicole was like as my boss. I told them about us being blackmailed for a night with my husband.

I said how I suspect Nicole was the one who's been calling me at night and sometimes during the day, breathing into the phone. I told them about the person outside my house that night, and how I think Nicole was involved in that as well.

I'm not sure if the cops believe me. I'm not sure how the cops truly feel about anything I've told them, because they've continued with their stone-cold stares for the past several hours of interviewing me.

Every now and then I've paused to make sure they were actually listening, because they gave no audible feedback. If someone had told me half of what I've been through recently, my mouth would be on the floor, gasping at every word.

After I told the detectives what happened, leading up to me going to Nicole's apartment, the bald detective wearing a bright red shirt finally says something.

"Do you hate Nicole Barrett?" he asks.

I look back at him in disbelief. What kind of a question was that? I don't exactly like Nicole. Is he insinuating something with his question?

"I did not like Nicole," I confirm. "She was blackmailing my husband and me. She used money and a promotion to try and get what she wanted."

The other detective, wearing a navy blue shirt, his sleeves rolled, raises an eyebrow. "Which was your husband?"

I nod. "That's right. I believe Nicole hired me because she knew who I was, Evan's wife. She wanted him back in her life and used me to get it."

"Who could corroborate this?" red shirt detective asks.

I take a moment to think and calm my nerves. "Well, I'm not too sure." It hits me, though. "Leigh. Leigh Olson. She was Nicole's executive assistant. When I was first hired, Nicole said it was Leigh who found me on LinkedIn, but I suspect that's not the case." I breathe out. "But she's been fired. Just the other day. I guess you detectives could find her though."

Blue shirt detective nods. "We'll look into this."

The other officer rubs his nose. "Has your husband been violent in the past?"

I breathe in deep. Do they not only suspect me in Nicole's death but Evan too?

"No, never," I say.

The detectives share a look. The one in the red shirt looks at me again. "Has he ever shared anything with you about any violence he may have committed?"

"No, never," I repeat. Evan told me Nicole jumped off the balcony, killing herself. Sure, he has an explosive mouth on him at times, but he's never done anything more than bark. He's never taken it further with anyone. "My husband's a good man."

"What about employment?" the detective in the blue shirt asks. "What has your husband been doing for work the past couple years?"

I lower my head. "Between jobs. He's not a very good employee." I explain to them about some of his past work history and how Evan told me he quit. For a moment I feel guilty when I tell them how he told one of his bosses to go F himself before leaving. I'm not exactly doing a good job giving them the picture of a harmless husband.

"Why did your husband and Nicole call off their engagement?" the bald detective asks.

I nod. "Well, Evan told me that the two had been very different people. They fought often." When I realize the implication of my comment, I quickly correct myself. "But that's what happens when relationships aren't doing well, of course."

"Did he ever report to you being violent or intimidating with Nicole?" the bald detective continues.

"No," I confirm.

The detective in the blue shirt opens a folder on the desk, takes out a photo and shows me the bruised arm of Nicole. The photo that she sent before she died.

"To your knowledge, this is the first time he's ever been violent towards a woman?" he asks.

"I don't... I don't know," I finally admit.

"You did receive this image attachment from Ms. Barrett, right?" he asks.

"I did," I say. I look at Nicole's red arm. At the top is the message she wrote to me: "This wasn't part of the deal!"

"What did Evan say when you went to the apartment?" the man in the blue shirt asks. "After, when you realized Ms. Barrett was dead, what was said?"

"I called the police immediately," I lie. I don't tell them how at first I thought the same thing they had. Evan had done something to her.

The two detectives share a look before the man in the blue shirt continues. "So, he didn't say that you should leave the apartment building before the police show?"

"No," I say quickly. The two share another look.

I don't need to read their mind to know that I'm burying myself. I immediately thought of the camera that was in the hallway. Perhaps it had sound to go along with what's recorded. Could it have pickled up on what Evan and I had said? "Okay," I say, lowering my head. "Evan did say we should get out of there, but we were scared. He told me he didn't do it."

"Do what?" the bald man asks.

I look at him as if he's stupid. "Kill Nicole! She jumped. Killed herself for being the miserable woman that she is!" The two detectives look at each other.

I start to think that I should have kept my mouth shut and not told these two cops everything. I should have gotten a lawyer. Now they're looking at me as if I all but confirmed that it was me who shoved Nicole Barrett off her balcony.

"I think that's all we need for tonight, Mrs. Walker," the man in the blue shirt says. The two detectives stand up, and not knowing what to do, I freeze. I half expect them to put handcuffs on me if I get off my chair.

"Can we go?" I ask.

The detective in the red shirt looks down at me. "We can arrange for you to get a ride home. Would you like that?"

I nod. "Thank you." I breathe in again. "Is Evan done speaking with you too?"

The two detectives glance at each other again before the man in the blue shirt speaks. "Mr. Walker, your husband, has been officially charged with the murder of Nicole Barrett." His words are as cold as ice.

I feel my world spinning. It's as if the small room is getting smaller, and I can barely breathe.

"You arrested him?" I finally manage to ask. "For murder?"

"That's right, Mrs. Walker," the bald detective in the red shirt says. "There's no easy way to tell you this, but he will not be coming home with you. We can arrange to drop you off with a family member if you prefer."

"I have no family out here," I say, breathless. I think of Tommy for a moment but don't bother telling them about my brother-in-law. All I want is for the room to stop spinning and for everything to make sense. "He didn't do it," I say, in my husband's defense. "He didn't kill her."

"How much do you know about your

husband's past?" the man in the blue shirt asks.

"What kind of question is that?" I ask. "Of course I know my husband's past."

He purses his lips and looks at his partner for a brief moment. "This isn't the first time he's killed someone."

CHAPTER 32

The detectives open the other interview room where I see Evan behind a desk, his arms stretched out, yawning. The man doesn't look like he has a care in the world. I've been nearly having a heart attack for the past several hours while Evan sits at a desk, drinking a soda.

I don't know who the person in front of me is, but it doesn't look like my husband. He doesn't look as frightened as I do after the questions I've answered.

When Evan sees me instead of the police walking into the room, he immediately stands up. "Alice!" he says, confused. "What are you— are you okay?"

"No!" I shout. "You've been lying to me."

"What?"

"You killed a man?"

Evan looks around the empty room. "Alice," he says, putting his hands down as if trying to get me to lower my voice. "We shouldn't talk about this here. We should wait until the lawyer is involved."

"You killed someone," I repeat.

"It's not what you think."

"You went to prison for murder. You never told me that! How could you? Don't you think that it would be important to tell your wife at some point in our life together? Were you ever going to say a word? You did it. You killed Nicole! Tell me now!"

Evan looks around the room again. "Stop, Alice. They're listening. Don't you know? Don't you see what they're doing?"

"I don't care what the police are doing! I don't care what's being recorded. You killed someone." I think of Nicole. "Two people!"

"No!" he shouts back. "It was manslaughter. That man."

I sigh in disbelief. "Do you even remember his name? How psychotic are you!"

"I know his damn name, Alice," he says sternly. When he catches his tone he calms himself. "Steve Moore. I was engaged to Nicole at the time. We were at a bar. This guy, I mean Steve, was drunk and belligerent. Kept flirting with Nicole right in front of me. I was heated, but I let it go. Tommy was there too. He wanted to fight him for me, but I got him to back off. I stayed on the other side of the bar after. At one point, though, Nicole's coming back with drinks in her hand, and Steve smacked her ass. She dropped the drinks and yelled at him. I immediately jumped in. We fought. I hit him hard. When he fell, he hit the side of a barstool. And—"

"Died," I say, completing the sentence.

"I was arrested that night," he says, taking a deep breath. "I got put in a room, just like this." He looks around. "I answered every question the cops asked. Every damn question." A tear is starting to form in his right eye. "And I spent a year in jail after the trial. Nicole left me almost immediately after I was officially arrested."

I breathe in deep. "Why didn't you tell me?"

"She was pregnant," he continues, lowering his head. "Nicole. She wasn't drinking, but she wanted to come to the bar with Tommy and me. She was four months pregnant. I should have never let her come to the bar. I don't know what I was thinking. After I killed that man, that night she miscarried."

Evan takes in a deep breath. "Nicole left me after that. It was my lawyer who told me she never wanted anything to do with me ever again. I never saw her again until I was at your office... After a year in prison, I wanted to leave. I couldn't stay in Ontario. When I left Toronto," he says between deep breaths, "I wanted to leave this all behind. What happened with Nicole, Steve, I couldn't even look at Tommy the same after what I did." He gazes at me, tears now rolling down his face. "I killed that man. He had a daughter, too. That little girl will go on forever without her father because of what I did. I couldn't bear it. I couldn't love myself anymore. I moved. And than I met you."

"You should have told me!" I shout, striking his shoulder. "I deserved to know."

"You did," he says. "You do. I wish I had. If I had told you on our first date, though, you would have left me. If I told you soon after, you would have too. What if we were engaged? You would have called it off, just like Nicole had. You're smart, just like she is— was." He lowers his head. "You would have seen me for the loser I was and left me too. I wouldn't blame you. I killed someone. There's no coming back from that. Everybody treats you different when they find out. Do you know how hard it was to ever find a job?"

I look at him, squinting, making all the connections now. "That's why you never worked?"

"I wanted to be a teacher, like Tommy," he sighs. "That dream died the same night—" He catches himself before completing the sentence. "I found a few jobs I liked, but eventually they wanted me to fill out information, or sometimes they would find out about my past. And that was it. Time to move on. The money I had for school, to become a teacher, it was useless at that point. I thought there was a quick way to turn that money into a success."

"You started gambling," I say.

He nods. "That only made things worse, much worse, but at times when I was at the tables, winning, I felt on top of the world. I thought I had control over my life again. Until all the money was gone. And then I nearly lost you as well."

I lower my head, trying to understand everything. It's information overload. Even though I can't understand how, it all makes sense now.

I look back at my husband, tears of my own now coming down my face. "You didn't have to kill her. Nicole. We could have left. You didn't have to kill her for us. That's why you did it, isn't it? To get her to leave us alone?"

He pauses a moment, looking around the room. "We should wait for the lawyer."

"Tell me the truth! This time, no more lies. I deserve it!"

He lowers his shoulders and takes a few moments before answering me. "I didn't kill Nicole. I promise on everything I care about. I didn't tell you about my past because I didn't want you to leave me. I didn't tell you about the gambling because that's what I used after I killed that man to feel whole again. I can't stop you from leaving now though." He paused a moment. "I'm not going back to jail. I can't! I didn't do it."

His bright eyes turn cold.

He gets closer to me, and the interview room door opens. The two detectives stand in front of me as Evan shouts, "I didn't do it!"

CHAPTER 33

Six months later.

Everything is different now. Everything.

Not only that, today is my husband's arraignment. Today he will officially put in his not guilty plea for killing Nicole Barrett.

There was no way for us to afford his bail to come home. There wasn't enough value in our house to put against it. Tommy didn't have that kind of money either. We couldn't afford a good lawyer. We had to take a court-appointed one.

It's been such a long time since that terrible night. The amount of media attention is finally starting to die down. It's nice.

With his trial starting soon, though, reporters and journalists will be back in droves. I understand why. It's a juicy story. A boss blackmailing an employee to sleep with her husband. A violent ex-murderer husband killing his wife's boss.

With the attention the media was giving Nicole's murder, the three of us were now famous.

Evan was right when he said how difficult it

was to find work after he had killed a man. What he had no idea of, though, was how hard it was going to be for the wife of a murderer to find work with him still in jail awaiting his trial.

As soon as I went into interviews, I could tell they knew who I was immediately. Despite me even using my maiden name on my resume, it was hard to get around people knowing what I looked like with my face plastered on news channels right next to a murdered woman and a killer husband.

Of course, the interviewers wouldn't say anything. I would go along with the interview, knowing I would never get a call back.

I couldn't walk into a fast-food chain for a management job without them knowing who I was.

Eventually I did find work, though, as a salesperson. I went from being executive of sales to being a salesperson for a small agricultural company. I had the privilege of selling the finest manure in Ontario. I literally went from being the top of my department to selling crap.

Despite the drastic change in my life, I actually enjoyed the work. Working with farmers was pleasant. If they knew who I was, they didn't seem to care. All they wanted was a good discount for their product.

Even though it was easy to make fun of myself for what I was now selling, I sold a good product that was important. I worked outside of

Toronto now, far away from all the urban people and the issues there.

My sales area was huge. I got to travel and speak with so many people. See so many different types of lifestyles. It was nice. Peaceful even.

Everything in the city was go go go. Here, I went at my own pace.

I was good at my sales job too. The owner knew what was happening with me, and despite that, we got along great. He never brought up Evan, unless I gave an update on his case. He was respectful of my privacy.

I live with Tommy now.

That's a whole story in itself. Tommy was also a colorful person. Rough around the edges at times. He could drink like a fish, especially during the summer. Living with him, though, I got to see a different side of him.

He was good at what he did as a gym teacher. He would tell me all his stories of what the children would do or say that day at school. It was truly hilarious.

His girlfriend, Vanessa, was a sweetheart. It's funny, there was a time Evan and I joked that she wasn't real. She was nothing but nice. A shoulder to lean on for me during a difficult time.

She's come over more and more the past few months. It's now at the point where she's basically living with us, and I'm thankful for it.

She's easy to talk to and has been so caring

and empathetic towards me for what I'm going through.

After the arrest, Tommy offered me to live with him, rent free, until I could sort myself out. It took a month staying at my house and facing bills I couldn't afford for me to take him up on his offer.

Not only that, but he finished the renovations on my house in a minimalistic way so that I could put it on the market. It sold nearly immediately and the new owners took possession quickly.

We lost money on the sale, of course. Realtor fees, and I promised to pay back Tommy for what he gave me to finish the renos. He said not to worry about it, but I do. I owe him, a lot.

Tommy and his girlfriend helped me move out of the house and into a small spare bedroom he had.

If it wasn't for my brother-in-law and Vanessa, I don't think I would have made it the past a few months.

It's funny how the people you don't suspect will be there for you come out the strongest when you need them the most.

My new boss allowed me to take a half a day off so that I could make it to the courtroom today. Tommy, Vanessa, and I sit in the front row.

Evan's lawyer sits alone at his desk, reviewing paperwork. He's young. Not much courtroom experience. There's not much we can do about it. To make things worse, Evan is making the young lawyer's life harder.

For the past few months, our lawyer has been trying to get my husband to accept a plea deal. The crown prosecutor offered ten years in prison for Evan pleading guilty to murdering Nicole.

He flat out rejected that.

He has stayed true to his story that he didn't kill Nicole, and I believe him. More and more I replayed what happened that night and the events leading up to it. The only true evidence the prosecutor has was a text of a bruised arm Nicole sent before killing herself.

That was going to be hard to explain. Nicole was exactly the type of person who would frame Evan before committing suicide though.

The problem? Convincing other people who never met a woman like Nicole.

Tommy thought his brother faced an uphill battle as well. We were all worried about Evan going to trial.

He could spend the rest of his life in prison if found guilty.

The doors open and policemen bring in Evan, wearing handcuffs, and he sits with his young lawyer.

Evan looks at me the entire time. He's not smiling. How could he? But even in his silence, I can see how happy he is to see me.

All I want is to run up and hug him and tell

him I believe him. Tell him everything will be okay, despite not knowing if that's true.

I give a thin smile towards him, while a tear rolls down my cheek.

Tommy raises his hand. "Love you, Evan!" One of the police officers in the courtroom asks him to be quiet. Tommy, being Tommy, ignores him. "We love you!" he shouts again.

His girlfriend puts an arm around Tommy and whispers something. Tommy nods and looks at me. "It's going to be okay," he says. "Evan's a fighter. He'll beat this one."

I sigh. This one? Meaning he lost his last murder trial. I don't respond, and instead look at Evan. He stares back at me. For a moment, it feels like it's just the two of us in the room until the back door opens and the judge comes into the room.

The judge addresses both the lawyers and the room. "I understand an agreement has taken place between you."

The defence attorney stands. "That's right, your honor. We would like to move forward with an official plea deal."

The judge faces my husband. "Mr. Evan Walker. You've been charged with the murder of Nicole Barrett. How do you plead?"

Evan continues to look at me as he lets the word roll from his lips. "Guilty." He lowers his head and looks back at me. "I had to!" he shouts. "I had to do it."

Tommy stands up in protest and begins shouting at his brother's lawyer. His girlfriend tries to calm him but is failing.

I continue to watch Evan. The two of us stare into each other's eyes. Without him saying the words, I know exactly what he's thinking.

"Please, don't leave me."

I wipe a tear from my eye as the judge pounds his gavel. "That's enough!" he shouts, calming the courtroom immediately.

CHAPTER 34

I drive around county roads, looking at my list of farmers' addresses my boss provided me with. I try to stick to my list of intended customers as they've shown interest in the past with my company, but sometimes find myself at the front door of an unknown barn or two.

I can't help it.

Sales is something I've always been naturally good at. I can't help giving a cold sales pitch to someone who has no clue who I am. I find that even with salt of the earth folk, the ones with the bold signs that say "No Soliciting", once I start talking with them, and relating to them, they are interested in my product.

I always ensure I give them a great introductory price, though. It's hard to turn down, especially at a time when everything costs more.

Today I'm about an hour and a half away from Toronto. It's an area of only a dozen or so farmers that have done business with my company, but some opportunities to speak with new customers.

After what happened yesterday at the arraignment, I want to take my mind off Evan and his pending prison sentence. A long drive and speaking with new customers is just what I need.

I get energy when I make a sale. Today, I've already made several.

My plan is working well.

After Evan was scuttled away by police in the courtroom, Tommy and I spoke with his attorney. At the last minute, Evan had had a change of heart and decided to accept the plea deal. He finally acknowledged that the risks were too high for him to refuse. There was a good chance he would have been sent to jail for the rest of his adult life.

Accepting a ten-year plea deal, he had a chance of getting out in time to spend the rest of his life with me. We could find happiness together in whatever living situation we could afford.

Kids were likely not going to be in our future. He would be in his forties when he was released from prison.

Management was now out of the question for me.

My life would forever be knocking on farmers' doors, selling them shit. The silver lining of that was I actually enjoyed it. For once in a long time, I didn't have non-stop feelings of self-doubt and insecurities bringing me down. I felt at peace vocationally, even though my life was in complete chaos.

I always thought I needed to be the very top of the business world to mean something. To make myself feel better. Worth something. Who would have guessed I'd finally find that with the job I have now?

If Evan was here, I'd be more than happy to give him a child, even though we would be broke and living with his brother.

Tommy continues to tell me that I can have the spare bedroom as long as I need it. I love him for that, but I can't continue to stay there.

The long drives around the county are a lot for me to do. I'd be better off living somewhere rural now. I always thought of myself as a city girl, but there's something romantic working in small communities and towns like I am now.

Evan would have loved it too. We could have owned a nice house in the country, with a large backyard. A large dog for that backyard. A nursery inside with a baby. It would have been beautiful.

Now, that dream is gone.

Sure, I could find a small place to rent out here, but it wouldn't be with Evan, at least not anytime soon.

I'm starting to hate the extra long drive I have as I go aimlessly looking for new customers. I turn on the radio, attempting to think of anything else, when something catches my attention outside.

A long rectangular sign by the side of the road makes my jaw literally open to the floor. I stop the car in the middle of the empty country road, looking in the rear-view mirror.

Putting my car in reverse, I drive back until I see the sign again.

"Brooks County. The Corn Capital of Canada."

Beside it is a symbol I've seen before. A corn on a cob. It was in a picture I saw in Nicole's office drawer. In it, she was younger.

Now I'm in that town. I drive forward, looking around. In that picture was a light blue farmhouse. I remember thinking how strange it was to see a blue barn, since many, I had always assumed, were red.

Now, working with farmers, I've seen many different colors and types of barns. The idea of a blue barn doesn't seem so strange. In a small area like Brooks County, it likely wouldn't be so hard to find, though.

My cell phone rings, and I pick it up. "Let It Grow, this is Alice." Thankfully, I don't have to answer my phone and repeat a stupid saying like Lovely Beauty Supplies had us do. "Have a Beautiful Day" is the last thing I think of now when I remember my former workplace.

"It's me," Tommy says in a hushed voice.

"What's wrong?" I say surprised. "Is it Evan? Is he okay?"

Tommy doesn't answer at first, and I repeat myself frantically.

"Yeah, he's fine, it's just, there's an investigator in my living room, and he wants to talk to you."

CHAPTER 35

When I get to Tommy's house, he's already at the front door, a look of concern on his face.

"He's in the living room," he says, gesturing behind him. "He asked to speak to you only and was willing to wait until you got home."

"Who is he?" I ask.

"He introduced himself as Investigator Hicks," he says. "Vanessa and I will be upstairs if you need us, okay?"

I nod and walk into Tommy's house. I look in the living room and see a large older man sitting in Tommy's favourite recliner. He stands up when I walk into the room.

"Mrs. Walker?" he asks. I nod and he extends his hand. "I'm Cormac Hicks."

I shake his hand. "Are you a detective, Mr. Hicks?"

"In a former life, yes," he says with a grin. He makes a clicking sound with his mouth. "Retired a few years ago. I'm a private investigator now."

For a moment, I sigh with relief. I was worried about what information a police officer would share with me today. Did something happen to Evan in prison? Was there more evidence against my husband? Was my life about to get somehow worse?

I believe my husband when he says he's innocent of Nicole's death. I don't think I could handle more tragic news.

Investigator Hicks smiles. "I'm here on behalf of the Olson family. I understand that you knew their daughter, Leigh, well."

"Leigh?" I say confused. "Well, we worked with each other for a few weeks. Is something wrong?"

"That's what the Olson family wants me to look into. They're quite concerned about their daughter's safety. She's been missing for some time."

I take in a breath. "Missing? How long?"

"It's been over six months," he says, making another clicking sound from the side of his mouth. "A missing person report has been filed with Toronto Police, but they've closed their file. They believe she isn't missing. She is, of course, an adult and can choose not to tell anyone where she is going or why she isn't contacting people she loves. The concern of course being why she would not tell anyone where she is, or why she left. Has she ever mentioned anything about leaving Toronto? Did she ever talk to you about places she would want to move to?"

I think hard about our coffee dates and meetups. “No, nothing I can think of. When was the last time anyone saw her?”

He takes out a notebook from his long jacket. “I was hoping you could help with that as well. Are you able to recall the last day you saw her?”

“It was at work, the day before she was terminated at Lovely Beauty Supplies.”

“Did you have any contact with her after that day? Text messages or calls from her, even if you didn’t pick up her call?”

I shake my head. At the time, I wasn’t worried about Leigh. Nicole was putting Evan and me in the worst position. Even after Nicole’s death, I thought about reaching out to Leigh, but my shame around what had happened stopped me.

“‘Is there anything you can share with me that you think could help my investigation?" he asks.

I shake my head. “Sadly, no. Does her family suspect something terrible? Foul play? Was there any indication that Leigh didn't move away?”

“None whatsoever. The last person who saw her alive was a night security guard at the building she worked at. He reported seeing her leave with a large suitcase that she was known for bringing with her. When talking to other staff at Lovely Beauty Supplies, they reported that she may have left for Vancouver. One staff member reported that Leigh had mentioned doing some modeling there.”

Mr. Hicks hands me a card from his pocket. "If you think of anything, please call me. Her family is concerned, as you can imagine."

He turns to leave but I stop him. "Why... Why was she fired?" I ask.

"That's another mystery." He makes a clicking sound again with the side of his mouth. "Your former boss," he says, being careful with his words, "she didn't keep a record as to why. We only have an email that was circulated the day after she was missing, confirming she was terminated. We could not locate her cell phone, laptop... The large suitcase she had the night she disappeared was not at her house. After she was fired, she vanished."

CHAPTER 36

After work, I'm visiting Evan at jail. Visiting hours are only until six. I'll have to end my day early to get to the prison on time. With the sales figures I'm bringing in, my new boss will be okay with me taking extra time to see him.

I never thought I would be a position to take time away from work to visit a husband in jail, but this is my life now.

It will be my first time seeing him since he pled guilty. He needs me more than ever.

My new boss is fine with me taking time off. I have to say, it's been great working for someone as supportive as he's been.

I look outside the window as I drive down the country road. I've heard the term "God's country" to explain what it feels like. It's true...

The farmland is broken up by large, wooded areas.

I'd like to say that I'm back in Brooks County again just to take in its beauty, but I'm not.

The visit from the investigator bothered me all night. I tossed and turned, thinking of what happened to Leigh. How can a young woman just vanish the way she did?

I looked on social media that night, trying to find anything I could. Of course, Investigator Hicks would likely have done the same initially.

All I found was a missing person announcement from her parents online. The post only had a handful of sad emojis on it and a few people commenting. Several shared the post. I clicked on the messages on the missing person post looking at what people left.

"We hope you find her!" someone had written. "Please be safe," another person said. "My condolences," someone wrote.

That bothered me.

Death is permanent. Being missing will forever make you wonder what happened to them. If I was a parent, it would be the worst imaginable fear, not knowing what happened to my daughter.

I don't know why, but I clicked on Leigh's mother's profile. She had her account set to private, but on her profile was a picture of Leigh as a teenager with her mother.

I could only imagine the distress her family is going through.

It was in the middle of the night that I nearly called the investigator. It felt foolish though. A small detail that doesn't matter. How could it?

The night Evan went to Nicole's building, I was in my office at LBS. I couldn't stay at home thinking about what my husband and Nicole might be doing.

I still hate myself for even agreeing to what Nicole wanted. It almost feels like a different woman actually allowed Evan to go to Nicole's apartment that night.

I push that thought aside and think about what happened at the office. In the bathroom, there was a red stain.

It could have been anything. I thought it was wine.

What if it was blood, though?

The investigator said the night security guard saw Leigh leave the building. So none of my thoughts are making sense. So what if there was a red stain in the bathroom?

In my mind, I continue to go back to the picture of Nicole outside the blue barn. Today, as I drive through the county, I haven't made a single sale. All I've done all day is search for that blue barn.

I know what it looks like and that it has the symbol of a corn cob on it. Surely I can find it.

How big can a county be?

The answer is surprising. It's huge. That picture was decades ago. Whoever owns it now could have repainted it. I've passed so much farmland today. I could have done so without knowing if it's been remodeled or torn down.

I think about knocking on every farmer's property. Someone's bound to know Nicole.

I hate myself for making my entire day about a woman who died months ago. A woman who in death framed my husband for taking her life.

The remains of Nicole that were left from her fall were cremated a long time ago, and yet even in death she had a way of living rent-free in my mind.

I turn down a road and pass a wooded area. I breathe in deep when I see it.

An old blue barn.

Beside it is a run-down looking house. I see no cars or trucks parked outside. No sign of life. I park at the side of the road and stare at the building.

CHAPTER 37

Nicole

Being dead isn't so bad.

I use a pitchfork to move hay around the barn. A chicken runs across my foot, and I smile.

That one I called Helen. I thought her white spots on her feathers made her stand out from the others. I liked her the best because she wasn't afraid to come close to me. I respected her moxy.

There's no news channels or cable for that matter out here. My Aunt Thelma didn't own a television. Instead she had shelves upon shelves of books. Romance books. Not my favourite genre, but it will do for now.

As far as I can tell, there's no internet connection anywhere out here as well. I can't see any cell towers nearby. A belt of trees surrounds the barn and my aunt's house.

I'm completely isolated out here, and I love it.

It's a simple life, and one that I can enjoy now. I sort of have to lay low. I can't exactly have a high-profile life anymore, unless I want to go to jail for the rest of it.

The white-color crimes I committed at LBS are one thing. After my meetings with the company's lawyers, I even thought there was still a way I could get away with the fraud I committed.

Murder is different.

I never intended to kill Leigh. I never thought I was capable of doing something like that. In the heat of the moment though, I did.

Leigh refused to do what I asked. She would no longer follow Alice or her husband around for me. She said she would expose me. Tell Alice what I was up to.

I couldn't let that happen.

In a fit of rage, I grabbed a large paperweight from Leigh's desk. It was one I gave to all employees. Printed in bold letters on the front was our company's saying, "Have a Beautiful Day." As Leigh blazingly defied me and started to leave, I ran up to her and struck her on the head. She fell immediately.

I panicked. She started to bleed. Worried, I dragged her into the bathroom, her moaning softly as I did, until I finished what I started.

As I watched the pool of blood from the open wounds in Leigh's skull pour onto the white tile, I washed my hands at the sink. It was only then, when the adrenaline of my actions started to wear off, that I truly realized how much trouble I was in.

I thought hard. I even considered calling the

police. What else could I do?

I didn't call the authorities. Thankfully, I was smarter than turning myself in.

Leaving the bathroom, and Leigh, I went to the janitors' closet, grabbing a bucket and mop. That's when I noticed Leigh's large luggage by her desk.

It was just the perfect size for her.

It took me some time to clean up, but after I did, I calmed myself again. That terrible night was not over. I had to leave the building with Leigh's body without getting caught.

How, though?

Leigh had her long scarf and hat at her desk. I put both of them on and said a quick prayer. Even better, in a cubicle nearby, someone had left a long grey jacket. I put it on and went to the elevator.

As I left the building, the night security guard called out to me and told me to have a good night. I didn't look back at him. Instead, I raised my hand and waved as the electronic doors opened. I would have run out of the building if I could, but Leigh's corpse was heavy to lug around, even with wheels on the luggage.

I brought her to my apartment, not knowing what else to do with a dead body. I put the case in my large walk-in closet.

It wasn't going to take long for people to notice Leigh missing. I realized my night was far from over. Wearing my disguise, I went to Leigh's house. I grabbed clothes and stuffed them in a garbage bag. I had already recovered her phone after she was dead. I spotted her laptop in her kitchen and grabbed that as well. There was no telling what information there could be on it. She could have some document somewhere talking about what I had her do. Some evidence that would point to me.

When I returned to my apartment, I showered and changed out of the clothes I had. Despite murdering someone, I was relatively clean, no matter how disgusting I felt.

I barely slept.

Instead I planned what to do next. I couldn't stay in my apartment much longer. I needed to leave. Go somewhere where I couldn't be found.

I thought of my aunt's farm. She was now in a nursing home. Nobody was on her property. The house was run-down, I knew. From my time growing up I knew there were few neighbors around.

It could be the perfect place to hole up until I could figure out what to do next.

I went to work the next day for appearances. Not only did I feel like a mess, I looked like one too. I'm not sure I ever looked as bad at work as I had that day. I regretted even coming in until I saw her.

Alice.

Seeing how distraught she looked that morning made me feel a little better. I confronted her. I nearly laughed when she told me that Evan was going to come over to my apartment that night.

I could spare some extra time before I was on the run for the rest of my life for one more night of pure adulterated fun.

Evan was going to make my day a little bit better.

I left the office and started preparing. First, I got money. Then I drove several hours north to my aunt's farm. I bought enough food that I not only stuffed her pantry but a large area of her basement with non-perishables as well. It would be enough food to get me through months of hiding.

Taking a quick drive around Brooks County, I knew it would be perfect for me. The nearest neighbor was ten minutes away by car.

I drove back to my apartment and got ready for Evan to arrive.

When he did, I was excited for our night, but that quickly changed. I was infuriated when he refused me. Even with threatening to destroy his wife's career and a huge sum of money, he wouldn't be with me.

All those years we spent together. The many times he willingly went to a bedroom with me, it all meant nothing.

We could have had a child together had he not killed that man. The stress of it caused me to miscarry. It was his fault I never had a life full of beautiful memories.

Instead, I left him. I moved on, and as my life was burning down around me, all I could think about was having Evan back. One more chance to have what I always wanted. I let my pursuit of a career get in the way of what could have been an amazing life.

It only took the fear of going to jail for fraud to realize it.

When Evan refused me that night, I knew my life was truly over. Even on the run, how happy could I really be?

I admit, I thought of truly jumping off that balcony. What was the point of continuing? What was the point of running? How long would it be until I was found and put in jail for my crimes?

I had murdered someone the night before. How much time did I have left as a free woman?

I wanted to jump. I did.

I thought of Alice and Evan moving on with life after I killed myself. The idea of their happiness was the only reason I didn't jump. I shut my bedroom door in Evan's face. He stood in the hallway, calling for me to open it so we could talk more.

Instead of doing that, I went into my walk-in closet. I looked at the case with Leigh inside.

As an executive, you have to think on your toes. Think outside the box to make it. You have to be creative. You also need a bit of luck.

I grabbed a belt in my closet and wrapped it around my upper arm, forcefully rubbing it as hard as I could until I could feel my flesh split. I quickly grabbed my cell phone from my nightstand and took a photo of what I had done to my arm.

I sent the picture to Alice, as well as a text. "This was not part of the deal!"

I went back into the closet and grabbed the luggage, hauling it to the balcony. I struggled to open the bag and drop Leigh's body over the edge, but was amazed at my strength in a time of crisis. I watched Leigh as her body flew down towards the little specks of people below. Before leaving, I dropped my cell phone along with her.

I heard Evan open my bedroom door, and I quickly ran out of sight along the balcony, dragging the empty case with me. The only other people who live on the top floor with me are the Rumfields, an older couple. Our patio shares a black rail.

I quickly jumped over it, and brought the bag with me. Still in my lingerie, I panicked as I passed my neighbors' windows. Thankfully, they didn't appear to be home. All the rooms were dark. The patio door was locked, and for a moment, I thought about jumping off the balcony for real this time.

I was trapped.

I tried to open every window until I found one that budged. When I got it fully opened, I snuck in the apartment. Once inside, I opened the patio door and brought the suitcase in. I stuffed it under a bed in a spare room.

Mrs. Rumfield has an impressive wardrobe as well. Not as nice as mine, but decent. Expensive. I packed up some of her more dressed-down clothes and stuffed them into a different bag I found in the large closet.

I was ready to leave the apartment.

How would I get to my aunt's farm, though?

I hadn't planned this out. I hadn't expected to do what I had with Leigh's body. It wasn't part of my plan to frame Evan for my murder.

That just happened naturally. I was surprised at how organically my plan had all come together, that was, until now.

The farm was several hours away. How could I get there?

This was, of course, why murderers get caught. They don't plan things through. I had been lucky up to that point, I knew.

As I walked towards the front door of the apartment, I tried to come up with ideas, until banging on the door startled me.

I shuffled my feet quietly across the floor and looked out into the hallway through the peephole. Alice was shouting. I could see her frantically banging on my door down the hall.

Evan opened my apartment door, and she went inside. He closed the door behind her.

I smiled to myself as I stared into the hall.

When I stepped back, I saw several hooks on

the wall. One of them had a pair of car keys. I grabbed them and left the apartment, and took the elevator straight down to the underground parking lot.

I shovel more hay around the barn, thinking about how wonderful that night went.

Sure, I didn't get to have Evan one more time or fix what I thought could be a beautiful life together. When he refused me, I knew that would never happen. After I killed Leigh, I knew it was impossible.

So, I did the next best thing. Frame my ex-fiancé for my death.

Oh, how I wish I had a working television. I would love to watch the headlines. I would love to see Evan with handcuffs on. His trial. I would love to see Alice's face when she realizes her perfect life is destroyed, just like mine was.

All I have out here in the middle of nowhere are my thoughts of joy that my death has caused... and romance books.

Life on a farm took some getting used to.

After a few days, I started getting bolder. I left the house and went for small hikes through the woods nearby. One day I met a couple in their late sixties hiking. They were my not so nearby neighbours.

I lied and said I was the new owner of the farm. They knew my aunt was likely going to sell the land soon and thankfully didn't ask too many questions.

They were a wonderful couple. I told them how I missed farm fresh eggs. They offered to sell me chickens. I bought four. The only one I cared to name was Helen.

Now I farm fresh eggs everyday.

They were planning on auctioning some cows soon as well. I told them I would pay a fair price for them if they would deliver the two cows to me. They agreed. Less hassle for them.

Now, I'm preparing the barn for my new animals. I laugh thinking that I could have a full working farm soon, with my own crops.

Sure, it was risky putting myself out in the public. The older couple seemed nice enough but all it took was for one of them to see a news headline and maybe they would make a connection.

They hadn't so far though.

I'm not sure what the next step in my life will be. Where will I go next? I try to take things day by day.

Right now, I can enjoy my simple life, with my chickens, and cows. I'll enjoy thinking of the urban life I ran away from and Evan rotting in a jail cell somewhere.

Every now and then, I hear cars pass out front on the country road. I hear one now, but this sounds different. It sounds closer.

I put the pitchfork against the wall and look out the small window.

My mouth literally drops when I spot her.

Alice Walker is standing on my aunt's front porch, knocking on the door.

CHAPTER 38

Alice

I knock on the front door of the house. No one answers. I wait another moment before knocking louder. Peering into the large front windows, I don't see much sign that anybody lives in the old house. It's pretty run-down. One window is even boarded up, completing the "nobody lives here" look.

When I peer inside, beside the couch, I spot a coffee mug and a book with a half naked man on the cover. It seems very much out of place for a home where nobody is there.

Someone has to be here. The only question is what to do if someone is.

"Hi, random stranger, but I know someone named Nicole Barrett lived here at one time… years ago."

Seems like a winning first line to greet someone mid-afternoon.

I look at my phone. I haven't made a single sale today or contacted anybody to attempt to make one. If my new boss could see me now, I wonder what he'd think?

I'm tempted to leave. Get back in my car and go. What's the point of being here anyway?

I knock one last time, praying that whoever is reading that raunchy-looking book is home to talk to me.

Nobody comes.

A sound from nearby startles me. It almost sounded like a can being struck. When I turn my head, I see the infamous blue barn. The same one that Nicole was standing in front of all those years ago.

The barn is even more dilapidated than the house.

One of the barn doors is slightly open. A small chicken with white spots on its feathers runs out of the barn. I nearly laugh at the oddity of it.

I'd wanted a sign of life but was hoping for one that I could have a conversation with.

I walk towards the barn, slowing as I near it. I look into the windows but can see nothing inside. No lights are on. No movement. Just a chicken. One that got away, as well. I look out into the field and see the chicken running, making a break for it.

"Hello?" I call out, as I approach the barn doors. "Is anybody there?" I stand outside the door, and call out again, but nobody answers. "My name is Alice. I'm a saleswoman." For a moment I think I hear the creak of movement inside. "I'm wondering if you're happy with your manure. Is your current provider meeting your needs?"

I roll my eyes at my own terrible sales pitch. Thankfully it's to no one, as I'm now certain the barn is empty.

Out of curiosity, I push the door slowly. It creaks until it's fully open. I peek through, and just as before, I see nobody inside. I do however see a chicken coop to the side of the barn.

"Hello?" I call out. I step inside. I see someone moving on the other side of the barn. Their back is turned to me. "Sorry if I scared you," I say with a smile. "I'm wondering if—"

"Leave me alone!" They turn and I see it's Nicole. She's alive. Standing in front of me with a look of pure evil etched on her wicked face. A machete is in her hand.

She shrieks as she runs towards me. From panic and confusion, I stare as my former boss sprints at me, the machete held back, ready to swing down.

I scream and run behind a wooden post. Nicole swings the machete, cutting deep enough into the thick column that she has trouble getting it out. She does though and pulls it back again.

"Nicole! Stop!" I shout. I run towards the barn door. She's right behind me, and I feel the wind from her swinging the knife. The machete slashes across my back, tearing my shirt and my skin. I scream in pain as I fall to the dirt floor. I drag myself to the barn door, trying to escape, but Nicole stands in front of me.

"How the hell did you find me?" she demands. "Who else knows?"

I stare up at Nicole. She looms over me, holding the machete in front of her face with both hands firmly gripping its handle.

"A private investigator," I lie. "He knows. He came to Tommy's house to talk to me." I think of the blood in the bathroom sink at LBS. I think of my missing friend. "We know you killed Leigh! You killed her at the office." As I make the connections quickly out loud, Nicole's mouth drops with each word, and so does the machete. It's nearly at her side as I continue. "You killed Leigh! It was her body that dropped from your balcony. Everyone knows!" Leaning against a wall close to me is a pitchfork. I quickly look at Nicole. "You don't know, do you? The police are looking for you."

Nicole smirks. "Looking for me?" I realize my mistake immediately. They will likely be my last. "So they don't know where I am, do they? Good bluff, Alice. You didn't sell me on your lie, though." She raises the machete over her head, but before she can crash it into me, I kick the side of her leg hard. I scurry to the wall, wincing in pain with each movement, and grab the pitchfork.

Without hesitating, I stick it out towards Nicole, making contact with her abdomen. I push as hard as I can into her as she screams in terror. I get my footing and rush forward, digging its points further into her.

Nicole drops the machete, screaming at the top of her lungs. Wide-eyed, I step backwards, and with as much force as I can, pull the pitchfork from her body with little resistance. Blood quickly stains her shirt and leaks down her thighs.

“Stop, Nicole!” I shout, attempting to reason with her. “Don't make me kill you.”

“I’m already dead.” She laughs, grimacing in pain. She wobbles towards me as I take a few steps backwards. She continues to smile wickedly at me, only this time I see bright red in her mouth. She spits out blood and coughs, taking another step towards me.

I raise the pitchfork to her again. She squints at me in pain, looking outside the barn door, and back at me.

“I hope you enjoy your happy life!” she shouts. “With your handsome husband! Someday you’ll have kids. You’ll have everything, but... you’ll never have what I did. You’ll never be like me. A boss. An executive. You’ll just be you. Alice Walker. A boring whore. A nobody. Nothing.”

I keep the pitchfork raised towards her, ready to stick in into her again at any moment. “Being nothing is better than being anything like you.”

Nicole’s smile fades, and she lowers her head. When she looks back up, I’m scared she’ll rush me again. One last ditch effort to kill me.

Instead, she turns and runs outside the barn. I lower my pitchfork in disbelief. I take a few moments to catch my breath before slowly leaving the barn.

Despite her wound, Nicole is already some distance away from me, running into the field behind the house. I watch as she runs through the field, into a thick belt of bushes, disappearing into the woods.

CHAPTER 39

Alice
Three years later

"I just want to thank you again for all of your business," I say into the telephone as I sit at my desk. "It means a lot to me that you trust Lovely Beauty Supplies with all your beauty needs." The woman on the phone is most certainly a happy customer and tells me she'll be calling back soon to talk about a larger order for her beauty supply store next month. Before the call ends, I quickly say our company moto, "And I hope you have a beautiful day." The woman thanks me again and ends the call.

I grin as I take off my headset. I stand up from my desk, staring out at the people who work for me. The new executive of sales, my former position, catches my stare, smiles and waves at me. I smile back.

Things have changed. I look back at my desk. It's the very same that Nicole Barrett used to sit at. I'm now the president of LBS.

Everything I ever wished for has come true.

I'm respected, looked up to. Lovely Beauty Supplies is doing much better under my leadership. Our sales have increased thirty percent since I took the position.

I turn back and look outside the glass walls of my office. The smile I'm wearing fades quickly when nobody is there. All the staff have vanished.

I'm completely alone. I look at the front reception desk, where Leigh used to sit. When I blink, my father is sitting there, a wicked smirk on his face. His mouth is moving. I don't have to hear him to know what he said.

Stupid girl.

My cell phone vibrates on my desk. I pick it up and before answering read that it's from an unknown caller.

"Hello?" I say as I answer the call. Nobody speaks. "Who is this?" I say in a panicked voice.

This time I hear something. Breathing. It's low at first but starts to quicken.

"Nicole?" I whisper.

"Have a beautiful day," her wicked voice shouts, before the call ends.

I sit up in my bed, out of breath, panicked. I can feel my pulse as my heart races. I look around the dark room.

I catch my breath before starting a grounding technique I learned. It's called 5,4,3,2,1. Name five things you see, four things you hear, three things you feel, two things you smell and one thing you taste. It feels weird going through the exercise, but it helps.

Finally I look beside me in the bed, at Evan. I'm hesitant to wake him. He's told me whenever I have nightmares, especially about Nicole, to let him know. He's told me he doesn't care what time it is.

There've been countless nights where he's been tied up with me for hours until I'm calm.

I don't need Evan to tell me everything will be okay. I know it will. I can calm myself now.

Lovely Beauty Supplies is in the past. I'm no longer employed by them and certainly would never accept any job there, even as president.

After what happened, I won a large settlement for everything that Nicole put Evan and me through.

It was more than enough to put us back on track. We bought a house in the country. Evan loves it. I love it. It's perfect for us.

It will be perfect for our child someday. I put a hand on my growing tummy. I remind myself of the beauty that's inside me. A little girl. We confirmed it a few weeks ago.

I still work for the manure company and still love it. It's not the job I ever pictured myself doing, but I enjoy it. It shows. The company's income has risen since the day I started. It doesn't mean too much with such a small team, but the owner made me head of sales.

He has even talked to me about buying into

the company to become an owner. I'm not sure if I want that, but I'm thinking about it.

Evan's doing much better as well. It took some time for him to figure out what he wanted to do for work. Now that he didn't have to hide his past from me, he was able to search for work openly.

I was surprised when he wanted to start his own renovation business. I suppose I shouldn't have been. It's the perfect job for him, and he can be his own boss. Tommy helps him during summer breaks and Evan even hired a young man to help him with his growing business.

Evan hasn't gambled since he lost all of our money. It was hard for him. He's open now with me as to what's going on in his head. I tell him what's going on in mine as well.

Therapy helped. It took him some time to agree to go. The only way he would is if I did the same.

PTSD, I've been told I have. I thought after all the time since the barn that I would be able to sleep better.

Therapy has helped me too. My nightmares are much less frequent. I'm coming up to the anniversary of when Nicole attacked me with the machete. It was a traumatic day, and my therapist has told me to expect my body to react on the anniversary of the event, even if in my mind, I know she's dead this time.

Is she though?

Her body was never found.

After she ran into the woods, I called 911 immediately. I even called the private investigator right after, as I waited for the police to arrive.

I was surprised when PI Hicks showed up at nearly the same time as the first police cruiser. A massive manhunt was undertaken. Dogs and even a helicopter were used. Despite the search, Nicole Barrett wasn't found.

I had no clue how far out the woods stretched. The day the police called off the search for her, I was scared. I demanded they keep looking. Her body had to be found.

The authorities agreed to one more day, and on that day they did find something.

Her clothes. All of them. Tossed amongst the bushes was the red-stained shirt Nicole was wearing the day she attacked me. Her pants were found. Everything. DNA later confirmed for certain that they were Nicole's clothes.

Why would Nicole tear off her clothes?

My mind raced with ideas. She must have found a new set of clothes. She could have discovered a hiker. Maybe they had spare clothes that she stole.

Nicole could still be out there somewhere.

I stand up from my bed and look outside, into the large backyard, into the woods behind it. I feel my pulse quicken, wondering if Nicole is watching me right now. I raise my cell phone and look at it.

At any moment I feel it could light up with an unknown caller attempting to reach me.

Nicole, breathing into the other end, wanting to let me know she's still out there. It's never happened though in real life but only my nightmares.

The police have different theories though. A doctor examined the bloody shirt and pants and concluded there was no way Nicole could have survived.

So why did she suddenly rip her clothes off and run naked into the woods?

The police had theories for that as well. It's not unheard of for someone to undress themself when they experience hypothermia. There are many stories of lost hikers freezing to death, and when their bodies are eventually discovered, being completely naked. The brain makes these people believe they are overheating when their body has lost nearly all heat.

The mind is a powerful thing, something I've learned after my PTSD diagnosis.

I remind myself that Nicole Barrett is dead. Police have closed the search for her body. Her corpse is somewhere out there in the woods, waiting to be discovered.

I know it. I hope it's true. That doesn't stop my mind from playing tricks on me. It doesn't stop the nightmares. I'm not sure if they will ever end.

Not until her body is found.

Until then, no matter how much I tell myself she's dead, I can't be completely at peace. I'll still jump when my cell phone rings. I'll sweat if I get a call from an unknown caller, sometimes not being able to pick up the phone at all.

Nicole was thought to be dead before, but she wasn't. What are the chances of her being alive now though? What's the chance that someone can be declared dead twice?

I try to calm myself, looking back at Evan nestled in our bedsheets, sound asleep. I put a hand on my tummy again and pray for me to be able to go back to bed.

I raise my phone again and stare at the black screen, waiting for it to light up with a call.

EPILOGUE

Sarah Penske

"Sarah!" James calls out to me in the dark. It's hard to hear over the torrential rain coming down in the woods around us. I'm shivering to death as the water pummels my body.

"I'm here," I say, calling out to my boyfriend in the dark. It's nearly pitch black. I can barely see what's in front of me.

"I found a cave!" he shouts.

My body shakes as I walk towards his voice, attempting not to trip over the bushes and long grass below me.

I would never have thought that my life could come to a swift end, at the age of twenty-five, just because I agreed to go on a stupid hike with my boyfriend.

James talked me into going off-trail. That was mistake number one.

He wanted to hike for a few hours to bring me to this beautiful waterfall that he had always talked about to me. When he was a kid, he was in these woods all the time. It was one of his favorite places to hike as a child. He said he knew a shortcut to get to the falls. That was mistake number two.

I can't count the mistakes that followed. Agreeing to hike in an area with no cell reception was another. Not telling anybody where we were going was even worse. It's been nearly eighteen hours since we started, and we have no clue where we are.

With rain pummeling us, and not being prepared for the harsh autumn weather, how much longer can we last?

Who will find us? Will they find us?

We're going to freeze to death out here. It's just a matter of time.

James grabs my hand. "Everything will be okay, Sarah," he tells me. His words are no comfort though. It's his damn fault I'm in this mess. I was stupid enough to agree to this hike. I had this crazy idea that he was going to propose to me in front of the falls.

We've been talking about marriage more and more, and today I thought he was finally going to show me he meant those words.

He rubs his hands on my sides, attempting to warm me. "Hurry," he says. "It will be warmer in the cave." He forcefully brings me up a hill and I finally see the opening.

Once we're inside the cave, I shudder more. I thought being out of the rain would be instantly better, but I almost feel colder.

James is as drenched as me, shaking in the cave. He holds me close and tries to warm my body with his. We shiver together in the dark as I look around.

"What about bears?" I say.

His teeth chatter as he laughs. "How many bear sightings have you heard of in this part of Ontario? It will be okay." He searches his wet jean pockets and takes out his lighter. He clicks on it until it thankfully ignites with a small flame.

"I just need to find some dry branches," he says, waving the lighter around us. "We can make a fire. Take off our wet clothes."

"We're going to die out here," I say, unable to tell if the wetness around my eyes is from the cold rain or my body.

"No," he says reassuringly. "No, we're going to be fine. We'll look back at this, years from now, and laugh at how terrible this was."

I sigh, wanting to yell at him, but hold back my rage. What's the point of being angry now? We need each other, especially if we plan to live. I hope he's right. I hope we look back at today and laugh at how near death we thought we were. Maybe this will somehow even make us closer as a couple.

That's after I murder him for being so stupid.

He lets go of me and starts wandering deeper into the cave. "James," I shout.

"It's fine," he says. "Just stay there. I'll be right back."

I shake uncontrollably as I watch him disappear into the darkness, only able to tell where he is from the dim glow of his lighter.

Out of fear, I want to yell at him to stop using it. He could burn all the fluid inside before we make a fire. If that happens, we won't survive the night.

Before I can tell him, James shouts, "Oh god!"

"What?" James doesn't answer. I walk towards the flame. "James, what is it?"

"No! Don't come here."

"Why?" I shout, confused, attempting to warm myself with my hands. In the dim light, I see James beside something large. "What is that? A dead animal? A dead bear?"

As I stand beside James and look at what he's found, I grip his hand tightly, holding my breath.

In front of us, leaning against the rock, are the skeletal remains of a person. Bits of dried flesh remain on some of its bones, reminding me that at one time it was a human being. It's fate, a reminder of what will surely be mine.

"Look," James says, raising the lighter at the rock above the remains.

Etched into the rock above is a phrase.

"Have a Beautiful Day."

* * *

I truly hope you enjoyed reading my story as much as I did creating it. As an indie author, what you think of my book is all I care about.

If you enjoyed my story, please take a moment to leave your review on the Amazon store. It would mean the world to me.

Thank you for reading, and I hope you join me next time.

Sincerely,
James

I'm always happy to receive
emails from readers at
jamescaineauthor@gmail.com.

Download My Free Book

If you would like to receive a FREE copy of my psychological thriller, The Affair, please email me at jamescaineauthor@gmail.com.

* * *

Now, please enjoy a sample of my book, The Jealous Wife.

THE JEALOUS WIFE

I have my dream job,
With a nightmare boss.

At first, Nicole Barret seemed
to be the perfect boss.

I was **dead** wrong.

It gets worse when I find out my husband knows her all too well. She's his **ex-fiancé.**

She won't let me quit without
destroying my career and my marriage.

It wasn't a coincidence that she hired me.

It won't be a coincidence if I disappear.

Please enjoy this sample of The Jealous Wife:

CHAPTER 1

Tomorrow everything will change.

I wake up to another perfect day in a small town.

I stretch, and immediately Lady, my miniature poodle, does the same on the bed beside me. She licks my face and I pet her white fur furiously.

Despite being alone now, I still sleep on the same side of the bed that I had when my husband slept beside me. A king bed for one woman was way too much, even for me. Lady made it easier though to not think about.

I hate to admit it, but sometimes I miss him.

I look at the happy face of my doggie to help change my mood. "Walk, Lady?" I shout enthusiastically, and her tail waves faster.

She watches me as I get changed into my athletic gear. Walking into my office next door, I grab the gold pendant necklace on my desk and place in in my pocket. It's bulky, and I don't like bringing it around with me on runs. It doesn't feel right wearing it around my neck either. Since I made the decision that will change everything in my life, I've been carrying the pendant more and more, and looking at the picture inside it, sometimes obsessively.

Lady watches me, turning her head.

I stretch out my arm further and do circles with my hands as I go down the spiraling staircase to my front foyer, while Lady scurries behind me, struggling with the steps.

Before I open the door, I stop at the small table near the entrance. On it were several pictures of Ryan and I, mostly while travelling. One from Italy. Another from our month-long trip to Spain. The best vacation we had was the one where we travelled to Fiji. The ocean was crystal blue. The beaches were serene. Beautiful was a word lacking the power needed to explain how amazing it was.

I glance at our Fiji photo on the beach, and at the vase beside it, where remains are kept. I read his name at the bottom of it. Ryan McDermott.

It's been nearly eight months since he passed. I let out a breath I didn't know I was holding.

It was a weird place to put my husband, on a table near the entrance of my home. It was almost as if he greeted anyone that would visit. Most people would have placed him above a mantle in a family room or maybe a bedroom. I hated the idea. Why put a dead person in a living area? Why would I want to remember that my husband was dead every night I slept or morning I woke?

After what happened, I tended to stay away from the living room entirely.

I was still in mourning of course. Some day, maybe I won't even keep his remains in the house. Maybe my ex-mother-in-law would want him. There comes a time where I need to- move on too.

What's an appropriate amount of time though? Thinking of Ryan can bring up loving memories, and a lot of anger. Sometimes I think I kept him at my home to torment myself.

I've heard gossip from my single friends in town that some of the men are waiting for their shot at the now widowed Kelly McDermott. I've already been approached a few times by male suitors looking to sweep me off my feet being that I'm vulnerable now. They probably hope that I'm some emotional mess after my husband died, but that's further from the truth.

I focus on myself even more than usual when I'm- down, or depressed. At thirty-one, my body is in its best shape of my life. Yoga twice a week. Strength training with light weights three times a week. A Zumba class. Pilates. Every morning, I have my run with Lady to start my day.

I look back at the large living room, with a tall brick fireplace that reaches the tall ceiling. The marble floors. The long dining table that Ryan and I used to entertain people at. This home was too large for one woman, and her dog. Someday I'll be ready to move on in life, but not yet.

Not until I get my revenge.

Tomorrow everything will change.

I smile, thinking of what will happen soon. The small town of Muskoka Lake is going to be getting a lot of attention soon. I- will be getting a lot of attention soon.

Lady barks, getting more impatient. I bend down and pat her head. "Sorry, girl," I say. "Got distracted." I grab the leash from the closet, and quickly put it on her. I make a kissing sound towards the vase as I open the front door. The sunshine blasts me in my face as I do.

It's nearly ten in the morning, nearly afternoon now. When you're single, unemployed and wealthy, waking up at an early time isn't exactly required. Ryan was the early bird. He was up, changed into his suit and out he door quicker than I took to place my feet out of bed.

I notice a White Escalade drive by, and the driver gawks at me. It was Dean Hemsbring. A neighbor a few blocks down. He was married with a young daughter, but that didn't stop him from staring at me like I was a piece of bacon waiting to be devoured. I wave back and smile. He sheepishly waves back and quickly turns his head.

I'm used to this type of attention, which I receive more now that Ryan is no longer here. I wonder what Evelyn Hemsbring, his wife who I sometimes have brunch with, would think of her husband's gaze?

I'm self aware that I'm pretty, beautiful even. Attention from men, and sometimes women, comes naturally without much effort from me to receive. I've grown accustomed to it. Dean is harmless. A man with an imagination who needed a reminder to not stare at the sun. He's probably more concerned if I would say something to Evelyn.

I won't, of course.

I close my front door. It's not locked. It never is. Crime is not a problem in Muskoka Lake. Everyone knows everybody. Some better than others. I feel I know every juicy gossip this town has to offer, which isn't much.

Lady walks beside me as we head down the block. I stare at the empty home beside mine. There are only three homes on our block. Each home is larger than the next, with massive front yards landscaped beautifully.

A white picket fence stretches across the property of the former home of Mr. and Mrs. Miller. The senior couple decided to move out of Muskoka Lake to southern Ontario to be closer to their grandchildren. They were great neighbours, who were always friendly to Ryan and me. I was sad to see them leave, until I found out who was to move in.

I break out into a jog, Lady keeping pace with me. I stare at the For Sale sign in front of the home, which now had a red sticker slapped across it. Sold.

The idea of new neighbors can cause many to become anxious. Who will they be? Will they be nice? Young children who will scream their heads off all day and night? Uncontrolled dogs who bark into the night?

Not me. I can't wait for them to move in. I know exactly who they are.

That's part of the benefits of being in a small town. Everyone knows everything. The realtor is a friend of mine from high school. When she sold the home, she was excited to tell me who my new neighbors would be, because one of them was someone I knew very well.

Nora Cameron. Now that she's apparently married, she goes by Nora Bowman.

My realtor friend had the assumption, like many, that Nora and I were the best of friends. That was never the case.

I stop running entirely as I get close to the driveway. Soon Nora and her husband would be moving in. It was going to be a happy day for them. Moving is always so busy, but exciting. It's the start of a new beginning.

I was happy when Ryan and I moved into our home. This is the best neighborhood in town, and wealthiest. Muskoka Lakes social elite live here.

Nora, like Ryan and I, must have done well for herself since leaving town.

I breath out. It was more like she ran away from here after what happened.

I grab the gold pendant necklace from my pocket, and open it, staring at the picture inside. What was a memory of best friends becoming a nightmare, not only for me, but this entire town.

It was time Nora got what she deserved.

Tomorrow- everything will change.

CHAPTER 2

Nora

I watch the two movers as they clumsily move a large sofa through our new homes entrance. I make a face as the padded side of the furniture thuds against one of the double doors. Thankfully it was the couch and not the wooden credenza that appears to be next when I peer into the back of the moving van.

My husband, Jameson, strolls behind me, wrapping his strong hand around my waist. He kisses the side of my face, his hand sliding to my belly. He's been more affectionate than usual now that I'm showing.

"I still can't believe this home is ours," I say.

Jameson kisses my cheek again. "When I saw the listing, I had to make an offer."

I smile, trying my best to not be upset at his comment. Buying a home is a huge decision, one that should be made together. Jameson, of course, decided to take it upon himself to make it all on his own. When he showed me pictures, my mouth dropped open at how gorgeous it was. I asked to set a time to see it in person, but he had told me not to worry, it was already ours. He had bought it before even talking to me.

He was so happy with himself that he couldn't understand why I was upset at first. I wanted to be included, of course.

It's a seller's market, he told me in response. Had he not made an offer the home would have sold to some other lucky couple the day it went on the market.

I couldn't get to upset. This was where I wanted to live the rest of my life with Jameson. Muskoka Lake was a beautiful small town that people often traveled to during the summer. The lake was only two blocks away.

This was my hometown, and I had always dreamed of returning, and because of Jameson, I'm back.

"Did I do right," he asked, kissing me again.

I had to give it to him. He had. The house was beyond beautiful. As soon as the real estate agent gave us the keys this morning, we immediately ran inside. The pictures didn't do the property justice.

I nod at Jameson. "You did. Thank you."

"Anything you want," he said.

Lately he had been overly affectionate at

tending to my needs. Jameson always wanted to be a father, and soon enough, that would be his reality.

No matter the time of night, he would tend to my random food cravings. Mcdonalds fries dipped in vanilla ice cream. Pickles with a side of peanut butter and toast. He was now banned from eating chicken anywhere near me because the smell instantly made me vomit, along with many other scents.

He understood though. He catered to me. It was endearing to see. He certainly wasn't like that when I wasn't pregnant, or even when we first started dating. Now that I was to be the mother of his child, things have changed.

The movers came back to the van, taking their time before attempting to lift the credenza. As they lifted it off the truck, Jameson now made a face of his own.

"I feel like I should have requested three movers now instead of two," he says with a grimace.

"Cheapo," I say under my breath. It was true of though, and he knew it. Jameson was good at saving a dollar but couldn't see the big picture sometimes. I told him some of our furnishings would be too much for only two people, but he vetoed me and only arranged for two.

I look back at my new home, and my annoyance quickly fades. When I was a kid growing up in Muskoka, I would come by this area, just to gawk at the beautiful homes. There were only a few other people living on the block. A large white picket fence divided the spaced properties.

It was truly a dream.

As the movers neared the entrance, one yelled at the other to pivot. The other moved and was yelled at to pivot the other way. As they entered the house another loud audible bang could be heard followed by one of the movers cursing.

"Okay," Jameson said. "I admit, three would have been better." I smiled at him. "At least I had the wisdom to find insured movers."

My phone rang in my jeans pocket, and I quickly took it out. "It's mom," I say looking at Jameson.

"Go ahead," Jameson said. "Talk to her."

"I can call her back when we get more settled."

Jameson waved me off. "This is why we're here Nora. We wanted to be closer to your mom when the baby comes. Talk to her. You know she wants to see you today now that you live less than ten minutes away."

I quickly hit the green button on my cell and put it to my ear. "Mom?"

"Eeeeee!" her high pitch voice screeches into the phone. I swing my arm out protecting my ear drum. Jameson smirks at me. "My little girl!" my mother screams. "My little girl is back home."

"Not so loud mom," I laugh.

"Sorry!" she says, quickly lowering her voice. "Sorry. How's the big day going?"

"Good, mom, good."

"Is Jameson tired from moving all day," she asked.

"No mom, we got movers. Jameson's not lifting a finger."

My husband makes a face. "Not true, Dorothy!" he shouts leaning towards my phone. "I'm very good at pointing my finger at where the movers should put things." Almost on cue we hear a loud bang come from instead of the house. Jameson curses to himself and points a finger at me. "I- should check on them."

"Yes, yes you should," I say in a deadpan voice.

My mom makes an overly loud sigh. "My girl is back home." The way she tells you would think I'm moving back into my parents home and not my own. "I can't wait to see you."

Finally getting to why she called. "I would love to see you today too, mom. Give us a few hours and come by anytime. We can order pizza."

"Eeeeeeee!" She shrieks again.

I cover my ear again and smile. Jameson was right again. This is why I'm back in Muskoka Lake. My mom was always the affectionate type, which was funny given how my father is.

I could already picture me and the baby going to grandma's house. Having picnics in the park together. Enjoying the beaches for an afternoon.

When we lived in Toronto everything felt- so distant. The buildings were darker. The people were all strangers. I hated it. I missed living in a small town. Now that he worked solely as a day trader working from home, we no longer had to live in a huge urban center like Toronto.

"Eeeeeee!" my mom shouted again after I didn't respond.

"I love being back in my hometown too, mom," I say. I put a hand on my belly, thinking of those images of my mom and my baby playing together in the future. There were many perks to us living near my mom with a newborn. Mom could come over, allowing me breaks to sneak in a shower, or give me time to nap.

My friends in Toronto were sad when I told them I was leaving to go back to my hometown, but those of my friends with children understood immediately why. Raising a baby can be hard. I'm not naive to what I have in store for me.

Jameson is the one completely romanticized by the idea of parenthood. I knew I had a lot of sleepless nights and grumpy days ahead of me. Days that would require a lot of patience.

Being back in Muskoka Lake made sense at this time in our lives.

"I'll see you soon, mom," I say.

"Dad and I bought baby gifts too," she

blurted out.

I hated it when she sent me gifts before the end of my first trimester. I was worried it would curse my pregnancy. I asked that she not send any more of them to me until I moved back home. Knowing my mom, she had already purchased enough toys and clothes to fill up this moving van.

“Thanks mom,” I say. “Maybe bring the gifts on a different day though.”

“Of course, of course. Just so you know, dad and I are going to shower your little girl with everything she wants like good grandparents do.”

That was another thing mom did. She is adamant that I’m having a girl. She said my belly is carrying higher as I’m starting to show more, which means a baby girl.

I’m not sure if that’s a myth or truth but- I feel strongly its a girl too.

Jameson and I liked to guess and talk about names, but we can't make up our minds yet. We can’t agree to any name for any sex.

We have our next ultrasound in a few weeks where we officially find out the sex. Once I see my baby on the x-ray, and find out what they’ll be, I hope I will have a better idea what to call it.

Jameson always tells me he couldn't care less what the sex will be, even though I know he has his heart set on a little boy. Whenever he talks about our child, he calls it a he, supposedly by accident. Jameson was the oldest of four siblings, all girls. Even his family dog was a female.

"I'll see you soon mom. Thanks for all the support. I can't wait to see you today."

"Love you, dear," she said in her high-pitched voice again. It wasn't exactly at her shrieking level pitch, but close to.

I end the call and place my phone back in my jeans pocket. I notice the front door of our neighbor open, and a young woman steps out onto the large wooden deck, with a small white dog. Her blond hair is tied with a pony that waves with every movement she makes. She's wearing a bright pink sports bra with shorts that are a little too short. She puts on her earbuds and touches the screen of her phone, before stepping down the stairs and beginning to jog towards me. Large dark sunglasses covered her eyes.

At that moment I realize I've been staring a little too long at her and look back at my home. It was hard not to notice her though. For a moment I hate myself for being envious of the woman's youth, and beauty. I put my hand on my belly, that's getting larger each week and try not to think what I'll look like when I'm nine months pregnant. I won't look like her anytime soon.

I certainly don't look like her now. After giving birth it takes time for the body to mend from the trauma of childbirth. All the genetics play against you when you want to look thinner again. One of my friends in particular had a hard time with the changes her body had after giving birth. She would always comment on the lose skin around her stomach.

Of course, she didn't regret having her child, but having a baby changes- everything, especially your body. I've been trying to come to grips with this myself lately. My whole life I've been petite. Not because of hard work, like the young woman about to jog past me, but mostly genetics. I got lucky. I could eat pizza everyday, soda pop, whatever, and for the most part it didn't show. I never really dieted before. Even when I was taking my medications, which tended to make people gain weight, I maintained mine.

With my peripheral vision I could see the young woman get closer. Her blond hair waving side to side faster as she picked up the pace, her dog attempting to keep up. Her face was stoic, and she appeared concentrated.

I wonder how old she is. Perhaps college age. Anyone who lives in this area in town is not struggling in life, so her parents must be well off.

It would be great when the time comes to have a babysitter live so close by. Although I'm sure my mom would be happy to take the brunt of watching over my baby, it would be nice if we could someday find a reliable sitter who lived nearby. Of course, it would take some time for me to trust anyone with my baby.

Jameson walked outside from our home,

waving his head with a slight look of concern. I wonder how much damage our reliable movers have made in our new home. I wave my head, sharing his expression.

Jameson walks towards me and notices the young woman running. Although he didn't stare at her for long, he spent more time than needed to notice a random person. The woman was clearly gorgeous, something that struck me immediately. It did bother me though that my husband appeared to have come to the same conclusion as well.

Maybe a babysitter gig was not in our neighbor's future.

I turn to look at the woman again and realize she's not as young as I first thought. Maybe it was the bright colors she wore or her figure, but her face is noticeably older. Maybe late twenties. Perhaps, older.

The woman smiles, and I notice a beauty mark above her lip.

Is that- no it couldn't be.

I smile and wave my head for even thinking about it and look back at Jameson.

Could it be though?

I look back at the woman. As if thinking the same, she slows down as she nears me, sliding the sunglasses off.

The smile vanishes from my face as the truth hits me.

She puts her head to the side and squints at

me.

"Nora?" she asks. Her voice is still as boisterous and confident as I remember.

I stare at her blankly, not responding. How am I supposed to react?

Kelly Van Patten is my new neighbor.

CHAPTER 3

Nora
Before

My best friend, Elizabeth Graham who sits in front of me in class, reaches around and places a folded note on my desk. I continue to stare at my English teacher, Mr. Johnson, who is blabbing about the writing assignment for the week, trying to not make it obvious.

Without alternating my gaze from the teacher, I quietly unfold it, taking a moment to stare down at its contents.

"Beach tonight?" it read. "Tap my back once for yes. Two no."

I smile, and gently knock on her back once. Suddenly another note comes flying behind her back a moment later, striking in my chest. A girl whose desk is beside mine covers her face to conceal her laugh.

I try to hold back my own as I quietly open the new message.

"We should invite Ryan McDermott."

I smile, taking a moment to peer at the back of the classroom where Ryan sat with her other football buddies. As usual they were chatting together, not paying attention to Mr. Johnson either. For a brief moment, Ryan catches my gaze and smiles back at me. He purses his lips together and blows a kiss and laughs with his friends.

His dark hair, effortlessly tousled, falls across his forehead in a way that makes my heart flutter. The way her leans back in his chair, exuding an air of confidence, draws me in like a magnet. There's an aura of mystery around him that I find irresistible.

Ryan's friend slaps five with him noticing the affect his air kiss had on me. The two of them laugh.

"Nora!" Mr. Johnson's deep voice boomed. I quickly turn back and look at him, straightening my posture. "Why don't you explain to the class the writing assignment instructions I just gave- please." He raises an eyebrow, waiting for my reply.

Beth, who always has my back, answers for me. "You want us to write a short essay on the themes of jealousy and envy that impacts the characters in Othello."

"That's correct Ms. Graham, but I asked Nora, didn't I?" Mr. Johnson walks down the aisle of desks towards mine.

Without regard for being caught I quickly scrunch up the note about Ryan and place it between my legs concealing it under my skirt. When Mr. Johnson looms over my desk he only finds the first note that Beth wrote. He picks it up and examines it.

"Beach tonight?" he says, with a laugh. "I don't suppose you and Mr. McDermott is planning on completing my writing assignment at the beach tonight, are you?"

The class erupts in laughter, Ryan's friends the loudest. I almost want to cover my ears in embarrassment, until I notice the look on Ryan McDermott's face. Even though the date was with Beth, Ryan's face seems welcoming.

Maybe we should invite Ryan McDermott to our beach night.

Of course, if that happened, and he made a move on me, Beth would be destroyed. She had a crush on him since grade school, even though he's never given her any attention to fuel her crush.

I look up at Mr. Johnson, pleading with my eyes for him to stop, and he catches on.

"No more love notes in my class, Nora," he says firmly. I don't bother arguing with him. I don't want to explain the note was from Beth. Instead, I give up and nod my head. He looks around the classroom with a smile. "This is the last month of high school- for most of you," he says, "try and keep what little attention spans you have left. We do have a final test coming that you will want to do well in."

A knock on the class door has everyone's attention. Mr. Johnson drops Beth's note back on my desk and opens it. "Can I help you?" he asks. I try to lean to the side as much as my desk allows, when I hear a young woman reply. I can't see anything though. Mr. Johnson's large body is covering the appearance of the mystery girl. "That's great, come on in- Kelly you said?"

Mr. Johnson turns back to the classroom, revealing a tall, thin girl with blond hair. Most female students at St. Joseph's Catholic High School tend to wear their skirts a little too low, and dress shirts more revealing. She was something else though. The skirt seems to barely cover her long legs. Her dress shirt had two or even three buttons undone, leaving little to the imagination of her cup size beneath.

It only takes a moment for one of the young men in the back of the class to holler something. I couldn't make it out what he said, but it was an obvious gesture that he was happy with the new girls' appearance. Some of the boys in the back laugh again and Mr. Johnson quiets them down quickly.

"Enough!" he shouts. "This is Kelly..."

"Van Patten," the girl says with a thin smile.

"Right, Kelly Van Patten," Mr. Johnson announces. "She just moved to Muskoka from Toronto." He turns to her. "Why don't you grab any empty desk."

Kelly nods her head, and looks around the room, spotting the one beside Beth. She quickly walks down the aisle and drops her backpack beside her.

"Hey," Kelly says to her. Beth waves back. "This spot open?" she asks, and she nods.

"I'm Beth," she says to her. "Did your family just move into the house on Meyers Street?

"That's right," Kelly says with a smile.

"I live down the block from you," Beth says, matching her smile.

Kelly lets out a laugh. "Well, you'll have to give me the low down on what's happening in this small town."

I hear chatter behind me. I turn and notice Ryan's friend whispering something in his ear. I see his gaze go across the room, but this time it's not on me. The new girl, Kelly, has his full attention.

I turn and watch the new girl continue to chat with my best friend. I watch them for a few moments before poking the new girls back.

She turns to me with a wry smile.

"Hi," I say, reaching out my hand. "I'm Nora."

Made in the USA
Las Vegas, NV
01 December 2023

81936341R00164